He paused and caught her gaze. "I mean, I do, but it's more a matter of politeness. With you, it's automatic. Almost like I was made to please you."

Laurel's eyes widened. "Stop that. I'll never be able to resist you if you don't stop saying such sweet things."

"Sweet isn't all you bring out in me," Deke warned quietly. "I have a whole range of feelings for you, and about you," he said, walking away from the steps and over to her. "At home, I usually felt very specific things for the women I dated. Some women I was attracted to. Others I liked as friends. But my feelings for you encompass all those things and more." He traced his finger along the line of her cheekbone, sending shivers of awareness through her.

excited about the challenge of proving to his family

Dear Reader,

As senior editor for the Silhouette Romance line, I'm lucky enough to get first peek at the stories we offer you each month. Each editor searches for stories with an emotional impact, that make us laugh or cry or feel tenderness and hope for a loving future. And we do this with *you*, the reader, in mind. We hope you continue to enjoy the variety each month as we take you from first love to forever....

Susan Meier's wonderful story of a hardworking single mom and the man who sweeps her off her feet is *Cinderella and the CEO*. In *The Boss's Baby Mistake*, Raye Morgan tells of a heroine who accidentally gets inseminated with her new boss's child! The fantasy stays alive with Carol Grace's *Fit for a Sheik* as a wedding planner's new client is more than she bargained for....

Valerie Parv always creates a strong alpha hero. In *Booties and the Beast*, Sam's the strong yet tender man. Julianna Morris's lighthearted yet emotional story *Meeting Megan Again* reunites two people who only *seem* mismatched. And finally Carolyn Greene's *An Eligible Bachelor* has a very special secondary character—along with a delightful hero and heroine!

Next month, look for our newest ROYALLY WED series with Stella Bagwell's *The Expectant Princess*. Marie Ferrarella astounds readers with *Rough Around the Edges*—her 100th title for Silhouette Books! And, of course, there will be more stories throughout the year chosen just for you.

Happy reading!

Mary-Theresa Hussey

Mary-Theresa Hussey
Senior Editor

Please address questions and book requests to:
Silhouette Reader Service
U.S.: 3010 Walden Ave., P.O. Box 1325, Buffalo, NY 14269
Canadian: P.O. Box 609, Fort Erie, Ont. L2A 5X3

Cinderella
and the CEO

SUSAN MEIER

SILHOUETTE *Romance*

Published by Silhouette Books

America's Publisher of Contemporary Romance

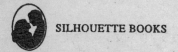

SILHOUETTE BOOKS

ISBN 0-373-19498-6

CINDERELLA AND THE CEO

Visit Silhouette at www.eHarlequin.com

Printed in U.S.A.

Books by Susan Meier

Silhouette Romance

Stand-in Mom #1022
Temporarily Hers #1109
Wife in Training #1184
Merry Christmas, Daddy #1192
*In Care of the Sheriff #1283
*Guess What? We're Married! #1338
Husband from 9 to 5 #1354
*The Rancher and the Heiress #1374
†The Baby Bequest #1420
†Bringing Up Babies #1427
†Oh, Babies! #1433
His Expectant Neighbor #1468
†Hunter's Vow #1487
Cinderella and the CEO #1498

*Texas Family Ties
†Brewster Baby Boom

Silhouette Desire

Take the Risk #567

SUSAN MEIER

has written category romances for Silhouette Romance and Silhouette Desire. A full-time writer, Susan has also been an employee of a major defense contractor, a columnist for a small newspaper and a division manager of a charitable organization. But her greatest joy in her life has always been her children, who constantly surprise and amaze her. Married for twenty years to her wonderful, understanding and gorgeous husband, Michael, Susan cherishes her roles as mother, wife, sister and friend, believing them to be life's real treasures. She not only cherishes those roles as gifts, she tries to convey the beauty and importance of loving relationships in her books.

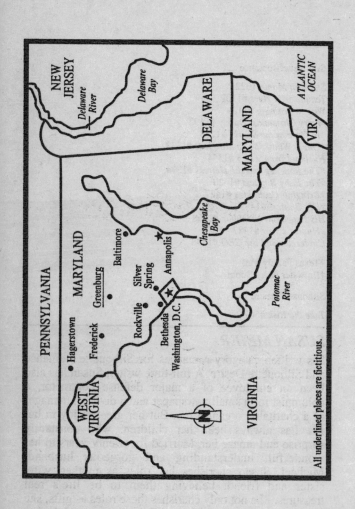

All underlined places are fictitious.

Chapter One

Deke Bertrim stopped his rental car in front of a simple Cape Cod house in Greenburg, a small blue-collar town in Maryland. On this sunny Sunday afternoon in May, bicycles and assorted toys littered the front yard, but the grass was trimmed and the flower beds were free of weeds. Though all the residences on this block appeared to be well maintained, the neat fieldstone-and-brick home was the best kept on the quiet street.

Deke breathed a silent sight of relief. The house belonged to L. Hillman, supervisor of the Shipping and Receiving Department at Graham Metals, and was to be Deke's residence for the next three months. Ostensibly he was here to go through executive training at the plant, but the truth was he would be investigating why the last audit of Graham Metals' books was off by more than three hundred thousand dollars. Though he hadn't said anything to his stepfather, he had been apprehensive about staying in the home of an employee, even if all the other executive trainees before him had done so because the rural Maryland plant was more than thirty miles from the nearest hotel. But seeing this well-kept house and the quiet neighborhood, Deke knew he had worried for nothing.

He got out of his car and grabbed his duffel bag and one suitcase. Considering the persona of an executive trainee, Deke had done what he supposed others before him had done. He'd packed light. He'd dressed down, wearing simple dark slacks and a comfortable polo shirt, and he would try to appear confident without being arrogant so Mr. Hillman and his family wouldn't be suspicious of him. As he scoured every nook and cranny of the factory, subtly interrogating the employees and even stealthily prying details from Mr. Hillman himself, he had to look like an executive trainee.

Striding up the sidewalk, Deke figured he had made a good start. In fact, he was so proud of himself for assuming a role completely foreign to him that he had to contain a grin when he rang the doorbell.

The stained-glass front door opened slowly. For ten seconds Deke only stared at the absolutely stunning woman who answered his ring. With the bikes in the yard, he was smart enough to guess L. Hillman was married. So that news flash wasn't what stole his breath or his power to think. This woman was gorgeous. Simply gorgeous.

"Hello. You must be Derrick Bertrim. I'm Laurel Hillman. Since you'll be staying here at my house for the next few months, I guess I'm something like your tour guide while you're in Maryland."

"Hi. Y-yes, I'm Derrick, but I go by Deke." He shook the hand Laurel extended as he mentally chastised himself for stuttering. He had met beautiful women before. Hell, he dated beautiful women. Seeing one out of context shouldn't short-circuit his brain like this. "It's nice to meet you, but you don't have to worry about showing me around. Once your husband directs me to the factory, I'll be fine on my own."

Laurel grimaced. "I'm sorry. I guess no one told you, but I don't have a husband. *I'm* L. Hillman. I'm the Shipping and Receiving supervisor at Graham Metals. I'm also the person who takes in the executive trainees."

Deke froze. When he'd agreed to this assignment, he thought he would be living with a grizzled old man and his family. Somebody with enough years at the plant that he had earned the position, and somebody with enough professional savvy that he did the favor of allowing executive trainees to room with him so they would remember him when they got to the top. He didn't have a clue he would be spending the next three months with a tall, thin woman with luscious auburn hair that curved at her shoulders and eyes so green Deke could see their color even though she stood in the shadow of her front door. Because the top two buttons of her white blouse were open, her long slender neck was exposed for his perusal. Well-worn jeans hugged her trim hips.

"Come in," she said, still smiling pleasantly as she opened the door of her home a little wider so he could enter.

"Thank you." Deke stepped into the foyer, carrying his duffel bag and suitcase, stifling the urge to loosen the collar of his shirt because he was incredibly uncomfortable and warm. Very very warm.

"Follow me," she said, and Deke nodded.

Okay, Deke thought, as Laurel led him down a corridor decorated with plants, wall hangings and knickknacks. *So he had to regroup.* No big deal. Lots of executives and plant supervisors were women. He didn't even have to think about that to know it wasn't an issue. The *issue* was that he was about to be *living with* this particular supervisor who was a woman, and hadn't she said she wasn't married?

Since every other executive trainee stayed here, Deke reminded himself that if there was a problem, it was his, not hers. She had already proved herself to be trustworthy, but more than that, no matter what curve this situation threw him, he had to handle it.

When they stepped into her spotless yellow-and-white kitchen, he said, "You have a beautiful home."

"Thank you. I like it," Laurel said, leading him past a round table surrounded by low-backed captain's chairs, then built-in maple cabinets with white countertops to a hidden stairway. "Let's take your things upstairs and I'll show you your room."

At the top of the steps, Laurel told him that he would use the bedroom on the right. She explained that the second-floor bathroom would be his and that the room across the hall with its lounge chair, television and desk, would also be at his disposal for the duration of his stay.

"You're giving me the entire second floor?"

"The company pays me a lot of money."

"I know, but this is your home," Deke protested.

Laurel only laughed. "This home belongs to the bank. The money I get for your stay here will pay down some of the principal on my mortgage, and I'll get the deed a lot sooner. I'm more than happy to let you use the entire second floor."

Studying her lovely, innocent face, guilt flooded Deke. Though it was necessary to covertly infiltrate the plant to discover the reason for the discrepancies detected during the last audit, he suddenly felt incredibly wrong about deceiving this woman. In fact, he felt like a criminal. It was the first time since his stepfather's assistant, Tom Baxter, created the plan to have Deke pretend to be an executive trainee that he realized he wouldn't simply be lying to an entire plant, he would also be taking advantage of someone in an extremely personal way. A woman, no less.

He wondered if that wasn't the real reason he became so flustered when he met her, and decided he wasn't so much attracted to her as guilt-ridden. His family didn't use, abuse or take advantage of anyone. If Deke was uncomfortable, overly warm and stuttering, it was because spying went against his beliefs.

Unfortunately neither he nor Tom could think of another way to ferret out the problem without alerting the person creating it and giving him or her time to cover his or her tracks.

"I don't need the entire second floor."

"Trust me. I have two young daughters. You will be happy for the sanctuary."

"I feel like I'm taking advantage of you."

"Well, don't," she said simply, and led him downstairs again. "I'm fine."

Deke heard a slight quiver in her voice, and intuition he didn't want to possess about this woman kicked in. She wasn't fine. Something was wrong in her life. Part of him considered that if he could ascertain her problem and fix it, he could return the favor she was unwittingly paying him and his family. The sense of guilt he felt would leave him. He could get on with his mission, and all would be right with the world again.

But he dismissed that because he didn't know for

sure she had a problem. He was only guessing. And if she did, he didn't know that he could fix it. Besides, it wasn't his intention to get too involved with her, the town or the plant. He simply wanted to figure out why the audit was off by so much money and get back to the corporate office where he belonged because he didn't have time for this. His stepfather, Roger Smith, planned to retire in two years, and in twenty-four short months, Deke would become responsible for the jobs of three thousand people and his family's fortune. Having spent the past ten years traveling the country, playing minor-league baseball, only working for Graham Industries in the off-season, he wasn't current with all the company's projects. And he wanted to be current. Actually he wanted to be brilliant.

No, the truth was his family *expected* him to be brilliant. And he always did what his family expected. If he had been older than thirteen when his father died, he would have taken over his mother's family's company right then and there. But he *had* only been thirteen, his grandfather hired the man his mother eventually married, and Deke got a two-decade reprieve. He worked summers for his stepfather, got the right schooling and even worked in the off-seasons while he amused himself with his passion for baseball. Still, everybody knew he would drop that when the time came, and everybody knew he would do what was expected. Because he always did.

Which was exactly why he was here in Maryland.

"Mother, is dinner ready?" Laurel called, leading Deke into the kitchen.

"Ready to be put on the table when you're ready to eat," the woman who was obviously Laurel's mother said. As tall as Laurel, with gray hair and the same fabulous green eyes, she stepped forward, wiping her hands in her apron as Deke and Laurel entered the kitchen.

"This is my mother, Judy Russell," Laurel said, introducing him. "And this is Deke Bertrim. Like the other trainees, Deke's agreed to stay with us while he's at Graham Metals."

"That's nice," Laurel's mother said. "You two want to set the table?"

"Yes," Deke agreed, jumping at the chance to help her because that was an easy way to pull his weight and maybe temper some of his uneasiness.

"That's okay. You take a seat," Laurel insisted when he followed her to a cupboard for dishes.

"But I want to help."

"I'm fine," Laurel said, pulling dishes from the shelf above her head.

He heard that damned quiver again, and felt the burden of guilt about not being honest with her when she seemed to have enough on her mind without his deception. Determined to silence the voice with good behavior and small favors, Deke reached for the stack of plates she held. Their hands inadvertently brushed, and an unexpected jolt of electricity sprinted up his arm. Confused, he stepped back. Seemingly unaffected, Laurel took the dishes through a swinging door that probably led to a dining room.

Deke leaned against the cabinet. Though he had relegated all his unusual feelings to guilt, there was no mistaking that jolt. It was sexual. Since he didn't really know her, he recognized that little zap of electricity probably didn't mean anything more than the fact that he was physically attracted to her. Which was fine. She was gorgeous. He'd already acknowledged that. He would probably worry more if he *wasn't* attracted to

her. But he was also a disciplined, intelligent man who
didn't do foolish things that would ruin his plans. A
physical attraction could easily be ignored.

"If you'll tell me where the glasses are, I'll be glad
to get them," Deke said, addressing Laurel's mother.

"Second door on the right," Judy said as Laurel
returned to the kitchen.

Though Deke was already at the cabinet, Laurel beat
him to the handle on the cupboard door. Again when
their fingers brushed, Deke felt a spiral of electricity
curl up his arm, and again he stepped back.

It was odd that his attempt to rationalize this attraction hadn't worked. Even his reminder that he wouldn't
let the attraction ruin his plan hadn't stopped it or di-
minished it. Which wasn't merely confusing, it was
weird. Usually he had no trouble controlling these
things.

He watched her move back and forth, to and from
the dining room as she set the table. He noted the swing
of her voluminous hair, then the swing of her hips as
she walked. He recognized and acknowledged he found
this woman very attractive, but he also told himself he
could handle it.

He had to. He had to work with her and live with
her for the next three months.

He narrowed his eyes and gave the problem his full
attention until the answer came to him. Having an entire floor to himself, he could simply keep his distance,
and that would work to a degree. But what he really
needed was a diversion, something to entertain him in
the downtime.

Now all he had to do was think of one.

As plates of food were being passed, Laurel surreptitiously studied the stranger she'd allowed into her

home. She'd had her suspicions about him from the moment she'd read his thin personnel file and discovered he was older than the typical trainee the corporate office sent to Graham Metals. But that was just the tip of the iceberg.

Because Deke's records didn't give her a clue about his personality or his lifestyle, except that he had attended Harvard and he got his late start in business because of playing professional baseball, Laurel wasn't going to offer him the opportunity to stay in her home. But Tom Baxter had insisted, assuring her that Deke Bertrim could be trusted. She'd reminded Tom that when she brought one of his trainees into her home, she literally *was* trusting him with her life and the lives of her daughters, but Tom stood fast. Deke Bertrim was not to be treated differently from the other trainees. Just because he was a little older—thirty-three—and a little better educated, that didn't make him better than the other executive candidates or change Tom's orders for putting him through his paces. Deke Bertrim needed this training the same as everybody else.

And he most definitely would not hurt her and her daughters, Tom assured her. Since Tom was a personal friend of Deke's family, he could state with unequivocal certainty that Deke Bertrim was harmless.

Peeking across the dinner table at her boarder's thick black hair, big blue eyes, broad shoulders, well-structured chest and beautiful biceps clearly outlined by his polo shirt, Laurel sincerely doubted the man was harmless. At least not to any red-blooded American female over the age of sixteen. But her daughters were four and eight, and she and her mother were clearly out of the market for romance, so she supposed the whole group of women was safe. Besides, she trusted Tom's judgment. In the three years and six manage-

ment trainees since she and Tom had started this procedure for indoctrinating his junior executives into the
real world of manufacturing, he'd never steered her
wrong. She and her family were thriving because of it.

"More soup, Mr. Bertrim?" Laurel's mother asked,
bringing Laurel back to the present and into the conversation around their dinner table.

"Thank you, Mrs. Russell, but I'm stuffed. That was
wonderful."

As usual, her mother beamed with pride. "My beef-
barley soup and homemade bread always win raves at
church functions."

"I don't doubt it," Deke agreed, smiling.

The guy hadn't wasted any time winning over her
mother, Laurel thought, then glanced at her two little
girls, Audra and Sophie. Staring at the new boarder
with sparkles in her blue eyes, four-year-old Sophie
was definitely enamored, which was okay since she
was well below the age of trouble.

But eight-year-old Audra was not even slightly smit-
ten. She appeared to be too caught up in anger to have
any feelings at all about the man at their table. Laurel's
beautiful brunette with the saucy smile and expressive
brown eyes looked about ready to kill someone. Laurel
supposed it was lucky Deke didn't have anything to do
with that.

"Audra, why don't you help me get dessert?" Laurel said, hoping to get some private time with her
daughter.

But Deke Bertrim almost jumped out of his seat.
"I'll help."

"We're fine," Laurel said politely, but firmly.

Unfortunately, he wouldn't take no for an answer.
"I still want to help."

"Actually I'd like a minute alone with Audra," Laurel explained, knowing that if they were all going to live together for the next few months, they might as well start being honest now.

"Okay," Judy said, rising from her seat. "Then Sophie, Deke and I will get the carrot cake. And you can have the dining room to yourselves while we're gone."

Sophie immediately hopped off her chair, not about to miss this golden opportunity to be nearly alone with Deke, as Deke snapped to Judy's aid, assisting her from her seat. Again, Laurel was struck by the fact that he was too nice, too helpful. But with angry Audra at her right, she didn't have time to puzzle it out.

"You okay?" Laurel asked the second the swinging door closed behind the merry band on its way to get cake.

"Mr. Marshall can't coach softball this year," Audra announced glumly.

Laurel bit her lower lip. "Honey, I know you really liked him," she said, smoothing the silky sable hair at Audra's temple. "But Mr. Marshall is getting old. If he retired it's because it's time," she said, trying to subtly convey the message to her little girl that he hadn't left because of something she had done.

"I know," Audra said with a sigh, then folded her arms on the table and laid her head atop them. "But he was the best coach."

"And I'll bet he thought you were the best player," Laurel agreed. "But I'm also sure somebody every bit as nice will take his place."

"That's just it," Audra said as the three amigos pushed through the swinging door carrying plates of carrot cake. "There's nobody who wants to take his place. Without a coach, we don't have a team."

"I see," Laurel said, hiding her concern. After Audra's father left, Audra had been quiet and reclusive until she discovered softball. Suddenly, with the introduction of team sports into her life, she'd become chipper and happy again. Laurel knew it was because Artie Marshall had taken a liking to Audra and treated her very well, filling her need for a father figure. But Laurel also recognized that Audra got her exercise, her connection to the community and her relief from summer boredom from that one little game. If Audra couldn't keep playing, there would be a big hole in her life.

"A coach for what?" Deke asked as he handed a piece of cake to Laurel at the same time that smiling Sophie handed a piece to Audra.

"Softball," Audra mumbled, obviously not as impressed with their new boarder as Sophie was, because she didn't even raise her head to look at him.

At Audra's lackluster response, Deke peered at Laurel.

Laurel shrugged. "This is a small town. Everybody works. Some people have two jobs. The former coach retired, but he's getting on in years. It must have become too much for him."

"Oh, Artie Marshall's just an old fuddy-duddy," Laurel's mother said, then slid a bite of cake into her mouth. "He's angry because he didn't win the championship last year and he's taking it out on the new kids this year."

"That's not true!" Audra immediately protested.

"I'm sure it's not true," Laurel quickly agreed, not wanting this to turn into any kind of negative commentary about Audra's hero. "And I'm also sure somebody else will come along."

"Like who?" Audra demanded.

"I don't know, honey," Laurel began, but Deke interrupted her.

"I could do it."

Judy's face bloomed with surprise, Sophie grinned cheerily, and even Audra lifted her head from her arms. But Laurel said, "I don't think so."

"Why not?" Deke said. "What else am I going to do? As a trainee, I only work eight hours a day. And I'm stuck in a town where I don't know anybody. I have plenty of time to do this."

Audra's big brown eyes grew even bigger. "You do?"

Deke smiled warmly. "Of course, I do."

Even as Laurel's suspicions about this very friendly, helpful man compounded, she couldn't deny that only a truly good person would volunteer to coach a bunch of eight-year-old girls. But more than that, his coaching the team would be a big favor to Laurel. Audra would always have a ride to and from her games and practices, which to a single mother was like manna from heaven.

Maybe she was wrong to be so suspicious of this guy? Maybe instead of questioning her good fortune with her handsome boarder, she should just thank her lucky stars?

Her brain immediately issued a firm warning that letting down her guard would be foolish, but Laurel ignored it. For once in her life it felt good to trust someone so easily. It felt good to get some help with her kids.

She couldn't think of a reason or a way in the world that his coaching a softball team could backfire. Still, she knew something would go wrong. That was just the way her life was.

Chapter Two

Since Deke was unfamiliar with the town, he accepted a ride to the plant with Laurel the next morning, but they hardly spoke. He spent most of the drive trying to get accustomed to seeing her in tight jeans, a loose ragged T-shirt and steel-toed boots. It didn't seem fair that a woman could look that good dressed that badly, and Deke convinced himself that was why he couldn't seem to pull his gaze away from her.

Forcing his eyes in the direction of the passenger-door window of her Toyota, he reminded himself that he was at this plant to find out how an audit could be off by over three hundred thousand dollars. At this point, he didn't know if someone had made an honest mistake, if someone had embezzled money or if someone was stealing inventory. He only knew regular procedures kept confirming the mistake without giving any clue as to a reason for it. Because he could very well be dealing with a thief, he couldn't be too cavalier about this problem or preoccupied with a pretty woman.

But he try as he might, he couldn't stop sneaking peeks at Laurel, and he knew he had been blessed that her daughter's softball team needed a coach. Since the season started in less than two weeks, he had been forced to call an emergency practice. Tonight he would be busy with a gaggle of eight-year-old girls, not six feet away from Laurel watching TV, smelling that wonderful scent she wore.

When they arrived at the factory, Laurel immediately showed him to the Human Resources Department. She introduced him to the director who would monitor his progress during his training, and Deke forgot all about his gorgeous landlady. He had passed the first hurdle in his charade, when Laurel accepted him as a trainee, but upper management might not be so easy to fool. As far as he was concerned, this was his real moment of truth.

Because Bertrim was the name of his mother's first husband and Deke's deceased father, and not the name of the stepfather who actually ran the corporation for his mother's family, Deke didn't give a second thought to anyone recognizing his name. And since he had played minor-league baseball for more than a decade, the Human Resources director didn't question his late start in business.

It almost seemed his unusual life was tailor-made to allow him to slip into a subsidiary unnoticed, and when he came to that conclusion, he got his first inkling that all this was awfully darned lucky—and coincidental.

Suddenly, it dawned on him that he had been set up. The realization hit him like a runaway fast ball. He wasn't sure if he had been sent here to actually get the training he was supposed to be pretending to get, or if he was being tested to see if he was smart enough to take over when his stepfather retired, but he did know he had been set up.

Insulted, furious, Deke didn't know what to do. He had worked for this corporation in one form or another since he was sixteen. True, he had never been at the top, but he knew the ins and outs...sort of. He didn't know everything. Even he admitted he should be at his stepfather's side every minute of the next two years.

All right, maybe he did need some training. But he didn't need this entry-level stuff. Besides, it was embarrassing. And time-consuming. Surely he could learn a hundred times more at his stepfather's side than he could learn from the supervisors at one little subsidiary.

Reining in his temper and his frustration, Deke became his usual controlled, disciplined self, not about to say or do anything out of line until he ascertained what was really going on. The HR director walked him to a section of the plant floor that was cordoned off by wire fence and looked like a cage. He led him through the mesh gate, called Laurel from a workstation at the back of the area and told Deke that this was his first stop in his working tour of the plant. *She* was the person who would provide his first four weeks of training.

Given the number of coincidences, Deke wasn't taking anything for granted anymore. Not even Laurel's easy acceptance. For all he knew she could be in on this scheme, too.

The thought that she might have conspired with his family brought him up short. He suddenly recognized that for the past twenty-four hours, while he had been blinded by her beauty and eagerly trying to think of ways to do right by her, she could very well have been taking notes on his abilities. Worse, through the course of the afternoon that followed, he suspected his performance was not worth writing home to mother about. He knew it for sure when he punched a hole in a bag of foam peanuts and sent them raining down on the entire department.

By the time four o'clock rolled around, Deke was so angry he could have spit nails. He didn't mind that Laurel had him doing menial labor, so he would understand the intricacies of her department, or even that he wasn't gifted as a shipper. It was the fact that no one talked with him about needing to be trained or needing to prove himself that bugged the hell out of him.

"So, ready to call it a day?" Laurel asked about ten minutes before quitting time.

Not sure how to deal with her, Deke rubbed his hand across the back of his neck. "Yeah, I'm ready."

Through no fault of Deke's they were within a foot of each other. Though he was preoccupied with not being told the truth why he was at this plant, he nonetheless had to steel himself against reacting to Laurel's alluring scent. He knew it would be total insanity to look into her sexy green eyes. But in shifting his gaze, he only succeeded in noticing that her complexion was smooth and clear. Radiant, in spite of eight hours in a grimy manufacturing plant.

"I heard you called a softball practice for after work," Laurel said.

Deke struggled not to growl with frustration. It was almost sacrilegious that his family would drag softball into their scheme.

"Yes, I did."

"Good. I'm sure the girls are eager to get started."

"Most of them are," Deke agreed, walking away because he didn't want to get any more involved with his "boss" than he had to. All things considered, she probably was the person who reported his progress to his family. And after the day he'd spent, running to keep up with tasks the other employees seemed to be able to do in their sleep, he doubted her account would be a good one.

But Laurel stopped him by touching his forearm. "I really appreciate your doing this."

Warmth radiated from the spot she touched on his arm, but more than that, her genuine smile of gratitude brought his thoughts to a crashing halt. How could he accuse her of being in on any kind of conspiracy? If she knew anything about his family's plan to test him, a woman of Laurel's level of sincerity would never be able to hide it from him.

Which meant she didn't know his family had probably paid the old coach to retire for a summer, and she really was appreciative of his coaching her daughter's softball team.

That knowledge inspired a burst of male pride in Deke. After hours of losing the battle with foam peanuts, pleasing her made him completely forget that she'd spent the day treating him like a peon. Worse, he had the urge to please her again.

Deke almost groaned. In thirty seconds of conversation and with one touch on his arm, Laurel made him forget he was here to please his family, not please her! How was he supposed to quickly, efficiently ascertain what his family wanted from him so he could do it and get the heck out of here, when the world's biggest distraction was always close enough to touch?

"You're welcome," he said, then walked away from her.

The truth was, this would be a lot easier if she was in on his family's scheme. At least then his anger would keep him sane. Without that, his wayward reactions to her could really throw a monkey wrench into things.

"All right, that's it for the day," Deke called to the noisy group of eight- and nine-year-old girls who were performing various softball drills on the grassy playing field. "Melody and Rachel, you gather the equipment this afternoon. Tomorrow we'll have a schedule of whose turn it is to make sure all the balls and bats get into the duffel bag for me to take home. I'll also have a printed practice schedule for your mothers. Right now, you guys, er, girls, can hit the showers."

Audra tugged on his pant leg. "We don't have showers, Mr. Bertrim."

"Okay, then," Deke said, glancing around to try to figure out what the appropriate dismissal line would be. "Go to your mother's car. Get on home. Get outa here," he said, and started to chuckle. This was different, but fun, and so far the girls were nothing but enthusiastic little charmers.

"See you, Mr. Bertrim," Sally Walker sang as she ran by him.

"See ya."

"See ya."

The chorus continued until all the girls were off the field and jogging toward the vehicles awaiting them in the gravel parking lot. Only Audra stayed behind.

Deke glanced down at her. "So, how'd I do?"

She shrugged. "Most of the girls like you because

you're cute. So you didn't do too bad, but tomorrow we're really going to want to play ball.''

"And you will,'' Deke agreed, picking up the duffel bag that contained the equipment and slinging it over his shoulder. The hour-and-a-half of exercise was exactly what he needed to clear his head and put everything into perspective. He was heir to the throne of his family's business, and apparently they thought he needed some training or a test of his abilities. He didn't like that he hadn't been told the truth, but he wasn't so arrogant that he wouldn't respect his family's wishes. Or Tom Baxter's. Because in two years Tom would be Deke's right-hand man. And Deke needed to win Tom's respect as much as he needed to win his stepfather's. After thinking all this through, Deke realized he *wanted* to prove himself. And quickly. So there would be no doubts.

And so he could get the hell home, away from the temptation of a woman who would drive him insane if he had to live with her for three long months. A woman whose daughter was currently yanking on his pant leg.

"But there's nothing wrong with some practice drills to get you into shape.''

Audra looked at him. "We're eight. All we *do* is exercise. We don't need to get in shape.''

Laughing because she was downright adorable, Deke ruffled her hair. "Smart little thing aren't you?''

"My mother had me tested to see if I was gifted.''

Deke stopped by his small white rental car, rifling in his pants pocket for his keys. "Are you?''

"Borderline,'' Audra said, shrugging. "But don't let that scare you.''

"Hey, I don't care if you have green hair. All I care

is that you catch the ball, throw the ball and hit the ball when you're supposed to."

Audra grinned. "Me, too."

Because the softball field was only a few blocks from Laurel's home, Audra and Deke made the trip in minutes. When he pulled the car into the driveway, Audra bounded out as if her pants were on fire. Deke followed her up the sidewalk and into the kitchen.

"So was it fun?" Laurel asked Audra, but she looked at Deke.

"It was great, Mom."

Deke smiled and nodded, confirming that the situation would probably work out. He saw Laurel breathe a sigh of relief.

"I made beef stew," Laurel announced, and as she said the words, Deke smelled the spicy, rich aroma. But he also smelled something else. Something sweet. Cinnamon.

"And an apple pie," she added, turning away from him to the stove, as if embarrassed to face him.

Instead of the sexual reaction he usually felt any time he was in Laurel's company, warm and fuzzy emotion enveloped Deke when he realized she'd made that pie for him...that's why she was embarrassed. Just from watching Audra play, he knew softball meant a great deal to her, and because Laurel was grateful to him for saving her daughter's summer, she'd baked him a pie.

Thrown off balance because no one had ever done something so personal, yet so practical for him, and he didn't know how to respond, Deke said, "I love pie."

She risked a peek at him. "Most people do."

"Thank you," Deke said, overwhelmed with a gratitude that felt very much like amazement. People had given him gold money clips encrusted in diamonds, but it wasn't the same as having somebody bake a pie for him. He got the sense that pleasing Laurel was the best thing in the world a man could do, but as soon as he got that feeling it amended itself. What he really felt wasn't that pleasing her was the best thing a *man* could do, but that pleasing her was somehow *his* job—or maybe his destiny.

Which was preposterous. He had a destiny all lined up, one that had been waiting for him since birth. He didn't need another one.

"You're welcome. Now go wash up and we'll eat."

"Yeah, wash up," Judy said with a laugh. "We're starving."

Deke hadn't even realized Judy was in the room until she spoke, and he knew this situation was throwing him for so much of a loop that he wasn't paying enough attention to what he was doing. If he didn't soon gather his wits and keep them, he might accidentally give away his real identity. And that wouldn't just be stupid, it would be trouble.

He left the kitchen quickly, scolding himself about keeping a tighter rein on his feelings and reactions. As he rinsed the grime off his face and hands, he reminded himself he had already acknowledged he found this woman dangerously attractive. He couldn't be noticing things like how generous and sweet she was, and he also couldn't be lingering on his own unexpected male need to please her. That would be pointless and absurd. Since he knew he was being tested, he had to be on his toes at all times, not constantly distracted by a woman he hardly knew.

When he entered the kitchen, he felt normal again. But in spite of the lectures he'd given himself, when

Laurel joined them at the table, he found himself stealing glances at her.

She was the strangest woman he'd ever met. Not strange as in weird, but strange as in different. She wasn't the pampered professional he saw during his stints in the corporate office. She worked in a manufacturing plant, in steel-toed boots and a hard hat. Yet, she still looked, smelled and baked like a woman. A really feminine woman. Someone who cared for and catered to her family. Someone who made him feel like family, too.

Deke was accustomed to getting special treatment, but Laurel wasn't treating him well because he was the son of the people who owned controlling interest in the stock of the company she worked for or even because he'd been voted Pittsburgh's most eligible bachelor three years in a row. She didn't know any of those things about him. She'd baked him a pie because she was a nice person, someone grateful to him for what he had done, not who he was.

The feeling that inspired was so appealing and so seductive he could have savored it all night. But he didn't because it once again undermined his control, making him vulnerable to saying something that might actually give away his identity.

And he couldn't say or do anything that would cause Laurel to guess who he was until he passed his test. He didn't doubt that he was sent here to figure out the reason for the audit discrepancy, *that* was the test. But as it stood right now, he didn't have a clue if he was looking for a thief, an accounting error or an embezzler as the answer to the riddle created by his parents. And his biggest worry was that it might take him more than the scheduled three months to figure it out.

But when he realized he might be here for more than three months, it didn't bother him as much as it had back at softball practice. The truth was, he sort of felt as if he had fallen into heaven. He had a challenge that would stimulate him for eight hours each day. When he left work, he drove to a ball field and literally got to play like an eight-year-old for two hours. And when he was done, he got a reward. Spicy, melt-in-your-mouth stew with dumplings and homemade apple pie.

Unable to help himself, Deke surreptitiously reached down and grabbed about a quarter inch of skin on his forearm and pinched. When it hurt, he knew he wasn't imagining this. The only problem was, he wasn't exactly sure he should enjoy it so much, either.

He expected Laurel to argue when he volunteered to help with the dishes, but she readily accepted his offer, because she needed to spend time supervising Audra's homework and getting Sophie ready for bed. While Judy filled the sink with warm soapy water, Deke cleared the table and found a dish towel. In fifteen minutes he and Judy had the kitchen cleaned and then Deke drove Judy to her home across town. He discovered that Laurel's mother was a widow, had been since Laurel was four, and that she had a slight heart problem that precluded her from working, so she baby-sat Laurel's kids after school and on their days off. Sometimes she came to Laurel's to care for the girls, though she preferred it when the girls came to her house. But the four of them always ate dinner together because they were family, and that was what family was supposed to do.

On the return trip Deke wondered if he'd landed on some distant planet where everything that happened was good and pure. Lost in thought, he nearly bumped

into Laurel in the downstairs hall, the little alcove
where the doors of the three bedrooms converged.

He caught her by the shoulders to steady her. Because she was wearing a sleeveless robe, the velvet
touch of her naked skin against his palm ricocheted
through him, and he remembered this situation had its
peril after all.

"What are you doing here?" she whispered, her
eyes huge because she had been frightened.

"I'm sorry. I promised Audra I would say good-
night."

When Laurel took a step back, trying to shrug out
of his hold, Deke realized he still had his hands on her
shoulders and quickly dropped them to his sides.

"Okay," she whispered. "But just peek in the door
and say good-night. If you actually go into her room,
she could talk for hours. And she needs her sleep."

"I'll just peek in," Deke agreed, lowering the vol-
ume of his voice, too. He didn't know what it was
about this woman that got to him, but she had something that could make him forget to do the simplest,
most logical things like lower his voice, almost as if
he couldn't think in her presence. Or maybe it was
more that when he was in her presence, he couldn't
think the way he was accustomed to thinking. All his
habitual thought processes slipped away as if everything was new. Her lack of pretense and artifice, her
treating him nicely when she didn't know who he was,
her appreciation for things he did actually made him
feel differently about himself.

But he also recognized something more. Something
physical that defied description. The woman was so
attractive to him that wanting to touch her was instinc-
tive. The most normal, most natural urge in the world.

And he had to struggle to control impulses he could normally quash with one rational thought.

He made a move to go around her, to get to Audra's room, but Laurel stepped in his path. He stopped, thinking she'd done that accidentally, but when she didn't move out of his way, Deke glanced down at her. She licked her lips and Deke's breath froze in his lungs. The woman was going to kill him if she didn't stop doing things like this.

"What?" he whispered harshly, desperately seeking any act of self-preservation.

She licked her lips again. "Look, I don't know how to say this, but...but Audra's very special."

"I know. And if you're worried that I'm somehow going to hurt her, don't. I'll keep the relationship centered around softball."

She stopped him just by catching his gaze. "I know. I trust you." She combed her fingers through her thick silky hair. "That's what bothers me. I seem to be able to trust you very easily. Very naturally. What I'm trying to say is thanks."

Again Deke was hit with a strange surge of emotion that completely defied description. It was warm. It was fuzzy. But it was deeper and more intense than a mere surface sentiment. He recognized the pride that filled him knowing he'd done something that obviously pleased Laurel, but that pride was edged aside by stronger, more potent, more important things. From what she'd said about trusting him easily and the way she seemed uncomfortable with it, he knew that she felt this instant attraction, too, and wasn't sure how to handle it either. He wasn't imagining this. He wasn't crazy.

"So, thanks," she finished, bringing him out of his reverie.

The soft feminine tone of her voice warmed him all over, even as it filled him with need. He swallowed. "You're welcome."

Another minute ticked by with Deke unable to do anything but stare at her, wondering what the heck he was supposed to do with all these brand-new feelings. Laurel was different from the women he knew. *Very* different. At home, she was also very different from the tough drill sergeant who ran the Shipping and Receiving Department for Graham Metals. He liked her. She liked him. But he didn't have a clue what he should do right now.

Pittsburgh's most eligible bachelor three years in a row absolutely, positively, definitely thought he should kiss her. But the guy who was supposed to become chairman of the board when his stepfather retired thought he should run like hell in the other direction. He had a big job ahead of him and Laurel Hillman was the kind of woman who could steal a man's soul. She was already distracting him from his purpose for being at her factory. He knew, beyond a shadow of a doubt, that getting involved with her would ultimately distract him from his destiny. She would change his life. And he didn't want to change his life. He liked it the way it was.

But there was no denying that he wanted to kiss her. No denying that he was curious about the feel of her lips against his and the taste of her mouth.

Still, looking into her big green eyes, Deke also knew he couldn't ignore the fact that a kiss would change things. And he couldn't afford that. He was excited about the challenge of proving to his family that he was completely, happily, shrewdly capable of running the family empire. But to do that he needed to be focused. He couldn't be distracted by a pretty woman or a romance.

He backed away. Laurel stepped to the side and he headed for Audra's room. "Good night," he said to Laurel, grabbing the door handle to open Audra's bedroom door. "Good night, Audra," he called, then closed the door and all but ran away from them.

"Good night," Laurel whispered, watching him go, touching her lips, confirming for Deke he had done the right thing. If he had kissed her, this situation would have probably spiraled out of control.

In her bedroom, Laurel bundled herself in her covers and tossed and turned for two hours.

She normally didn't do things like this. She normally didn't want to kiss her boarder. But this time she wanted to.

She really wanted to.

And it scared the life out of her.

Chapter Three

The alarm woke Laurel the next morning, and though she quickly silenced it because she didn't want an ebullient four-year-old girl bouncing into her room, she didn't get out of bed. Instead, she pulled her comforter over her head and squeezed her eyes shut.

She would have let that man kiss her last night. A virtual stranger. Another man on the fast track. Heck, she would have happily kissed him first if she thought she could stretch far enough, quickly enough, to reach his mouth before he changed his mind and turned away.

She knew better than this. That was why she was so comfortable taking in executive-trainee boarders. Her ex-husband had been a well-educated man on the fast track, a man who was working his way to upper management in leaps and bounds, rather than one rung on the corporate ladder at a time. But when Aaron got his big break, a job as president of a manufacturing plant in Texas, he told her that she and Audra didn't fit into the world he was entering. So he'd left them. The day she discovered she was pregnant with Sophie, he'd left them with a mortgage, a used car and not even grocery money in the bank.

She filed for child support, and instead of giving it, Aaron waived his rights to the kids. Completely. He had never even seen Sophie. He no longer acknowledged his daughters' existence, and if the gossip she heard was true, he now had another wife, more kids. Two boys this time. And a corporate-lawyer wife. A woman who made as much money as he did, someone who enhanced his position.

Yeah, Laurel knew all about executive trainees. She didn't belong in their world, and they were only passing through hers. She saw the situation for what it was. If she developed anything other than friendship with any one of these guys, she would be walking irresponsibly into another heartbreak.

Grounded by those realities, Laurel climbed out of bed. Though it was a warm May morning, she slid out of her sleeveless pajamas and put on a one-piece, long-sleeved flannel pair that even had feet, then covered them with a chenille robe. In case Deke had gotten the wrong idea the night before from her concealing, but more flattering summer-weight nightclothes, she nipped that problem in the bud.

She went to the kitchen and retrieved a filter and ground coffee to make a pot so it would be ready when she got out of the shower. Unfortunately, when she turned from the cabinet to go back to her bedroom, her executive-trainee border was already in the kitchen doorway. Their eyes met for a few seconds, and then Deke's gaze sort of tumbled from her sleep-tousled hair to her thick robe, to the legs and feet of her flannel pajamas.

Red flannel pajamas. Sprinkled with Santas. Covered by a robe so thick it could be a winter coat.

She probably looked like an idiot.

"Hey, Pajama Mama!"

Grateful for the interruption, Laurel turned toward the alcove door. "Hey, Sophia Maria," she said, stooping and opening her arms to let blue-eyed, blond-haired Sophie jump inside for a hug.

"Are you gonna make me pancakes?" Sophie asked energetically before she gave Laurel a smacking kiss on the cheek.

"Do you want pancakes?"

Grinning happily, Sophie nodded.

"Then pancakes it is," Laurel said, sliding her four-year-old daughter onto one of the captain's chairs at the table. "Right after I shower."

Accustomed to little delays and disruptions, Sophie again nodded her agreement.

After a hasty "Good morning. Help yourself to coffee when it's ready" to Deke, Laurel scrambled out of the kitchen and into her bedroom.

When she returned a few minutes later, showered and dressed in jeans and another old T-shirt, Deke and Sophie were already eating. Laurel stopped dead in her tracks.

"I hope you don't mind," Deke said, indicating the pancakes with his fork. "Sophie and I were a little hungry."

"No. No, that's fine," Laurel said, barely able to keep the astonishment out of her voice.

Deke winced. "You don't sound like it's fine."

"I'm just surprised," Laurel said, taking a seat at

the table and fixing a plate of pancakes for herself.
"The boarders I've taken in usually don't cook."

"Lots of small-town minor-league teams like to have
their players room with people in the community. It's
good PR," Deke explained, then took a bite of pan-
cake. After he chewed and swallowed, he added, "But
we weren't supposed to let our hosts wait on us. We
were supposed to try to blend in like family. That's
when I learned how to cook."

"So you're used to being a boarder?"

He shook his head. "Yes and no. I only did it twice,
and both families I was assigned to had schedules that
conflicted with mine—"

"Hey, Deke!" Audra said, entering the room. Laurel's eight-year-old was self-sufficient to the point that
she always had herself dressed for school before she
came into the kitchen for breakfast. Her sleeveless shirt
and jeans made her look too thin and too young to be
as independent as she was.

"Hey, Audra. Ready for practice this afternoon?"

"Yeah. You make our schedule?"

"Yeah. You practice that overhand throw I showed
you?"

"Yeah."

From there the conversation turned to the softball
team. With Deke and Audra talking like longtime
friends, and with him having made breakfast for starving Sophie, Laurel knew beyond a shadow of a doubt
that this particular fast-tracking executive trainee was
nothing like the other men she had housed. Certainly
not like her ex-husband.

In fact, he was so unlike her usual guests that she
was having trouble equating him with her ex-husband,
and that, she realized, was the problem. She wasn't a

stupid woman, but she wasn't a blind one, either. The man was gorgeous. And different. Not only was he good to Sophie and right for Audra, but he could cook. None of her executive trainees had ever—*ever*—volunteered to cook. She could think of only one who had even made a pot of coffee.

Laurel was losing her natural defenses, and she decided the best way to combat the latest assault on her conviction to stay away from him was the direct approach. Surely there was *something* wrong with this guy. Something in his past that would make him much less desirable. Once she found out what that was, she would be safe again. And because every female in the plant had been asking her questions about him, she knew exactly how to unearth it quickly, easily and so painfully he would stop giving her those sidelong glances that clearly let her know he found her attractive, red Santa pajamas and all.

Since Deke now drove himself to work, Laurel waited until they were well into the morning routine and the other Shipping and Receiving employees were occupied with their jobs in different sections of the cage before she confronted him.

"So, Deke," she said, standing beside his desk and feigning interest in the stack of documents in front of him, "you have me completely baffled." Pretending to be occupied with checking his workload, she asked, "How does an absolutely gorgeous man who can cook get to be thirty-three without getting married?"

Her description made Deke laugh, though he wasn't surprised she asked. After that little rendezvous in the alcove the night before, neither of them could act as if they didn't find the other attractive. And straightforward Laurel wouldn't beat around the bush. Just like with those ridiculous pajamas, she would find the fastest—never mind most embarrassing—way to diffuse this problem.

"I guess I've never wanted to get married," he said, glancing up at her.

Looking at her expectant face, he wished the eagerness he saw in her eyes meant that she had changed her mind about their situation and was anticipating he would tell her something that would give her the green light to pursue the attraction. But he knew better. Laurel was too practical, too blunt, too pragmatic, too honest. If she wanted to pursue him, she would just do it. She wouldn't ask permission.

Disappointment flooded him, but he ignored it. "As silly as this is going to sound..." he began, sorting through some packing slips on his desk and feeling that they should try whatever means available to diminish the attraction. It was imprudent and irresponsible to be unhappy that she had somehow made up her mind he wasn't worth pursuing. No matter how much electricity sizzled between them, they couldn't have a relationship. There was no sense in being dumb about this.

"...for every one of the ten years I played minor-league ball, I thought I was going to be picked up by a major-league team." He paused, looked into her eyes again and wasn't surprised when the click of their gazes caused his pulse to pick up.

In fact, since she was being so strong, he decided he could relax a little and enjoy the surge of excitement just being near her gave him. Unfortunately that quickly turned into the need for a kiss, and he found himself wanting to press his palms to her cheeks, to bring her face to his so he could feel the softness of her mouth against his. Though he knew he would never kiss her in a million years, somehow the longing, the wanting, was its own reward, and he let himself savor that, too.

"But I never got the big call. I never came out of the minor leagues. I would probably still be there now, except my stepfather—"

Deke stopped himself, face-to-face with the problem he had been worrying about all along. His preoccupation with her had almost caused him to make a monumental slip. He couldn't afford any kind of mental lapse. He was supposed to be sharp. Investigating. Not taking advantage of her discipline so he could enjoy feelings and sensations he wasn't supposed to have.

"Your stepfather what?"

He drew a long breath and returned his attention to assembling the tasks on his desk. "My stepfather convinced me that I should find a more stable job."

Laurel shrugged. "He was probably right."

For the first time Deke admitted to himself that he wasn't sure he agreed. He wanted to take over the company. He wanted his stepfather to retire and enjoy what was left of his life. But Deke missed baseball. He missed that piece of his identity; there was a part of him that felt empty and lost without it. Business gave him purpose and responsibilities, but baseball had given him heart, and maybe a soul. Coaching the girls provided a little relief, but not enough, and he still felt the loss. Part of him now wondered if that wasn't why he was so drawn to Laurel.

"But that doesn't explain why you've never married. Was it because you thought no woman would want to be stuck with a man who traveled around the country playing sports? Or did you refuse to tie yourself down to one woman?"

Deke only stared at her. Because he had taken a long mental side trip, he wasn't surprised she'd dragged him back into the conversation. But he hadn't expected her to be so desperate to be rid of him that she would be brutally blunt. "You really don't mince words, do you?"

"I can't," Laurel said, then dropped a stack of green papers onto the desk in front of him. "I've already gotten a million questions from the girls at break time. Tomorrow is our one-hour lunch. I won't survive if I don't have some details to give them."

"Oh," Deke said, suddenly feeling foolish. She was asking for her friends? He couldn't believe he'd misinterpreted her intentions. He knew she found him attractive. He also knew from those pajamas that she didn't want to find him attractive. Still, her reason for probing made more sense than to think she was so determined to be rid of him she would be rude. She wasn't rude. She was sweet and kind and deliciously wonderful.

Which was exactly why he had to stay the hell away from her. Rude he could combat. Sweet, sensitive and considerate made him want to confide in her. Trust her. And that was the bottom-line problem. He *wanted* to trust her. But he couldn't. He couldn't trust anybody. Especially not the woman who might know exactly why Tom Baxter had sent him to this tiny factory on the edge of nowhere.

The crazy part of it was, if he told her the truth about why he hadn't married, their chemistry wouldn't be a problem anymore, because she would stay away from him. She might even stop being nice to him—which would probably take away his desire to confide in her.

Suddenly he realized the truth would set them both free.

"I haven't gotten married because I don't think I'm a good candidate for marriage. I've always been very happy with my life exactly the way it is. I'm free to do what I want to do when I want to do it." *And free to take over when my stepfather stops working. No worry that I'm shortchanging a wife, no commitments to consider, no complications. Just a clear path to do what was required as heir to the Graham fortune.* Getting married had never once entered his head because it would have confused things.

"I can't understand why anyone would voluntarily make a commitment like marriage," he added, so honest even he felt like a heel. "Except to have kids," he decided on the spot. "I never realized how much I liked kids until I started coaching your daughter's softball team."

"Well, they certainly love you," Laurel stated emphatically, then turned her attention to the green papers on his desk. "Anyway, these are purchase orders," she said, realizing she had dodged a bullet by making that quick decision the night before not to kiss him. Just like her first husband, Deke Bertrim wasn't right for her. He might not be the kind who would pick a wife to enhance his career, but in some respects his reasons for not getting married were actually more deadly. He was self-centered, self-absorbed and unable to commit.

Thank God. Now they could get on with the rest of his training.

"Purchase orders are issued by the Purchasing Department when they buy goods and supplies. So, every time something comes through that door," she said, pointing to the Shipping and Receiving bay, "we should be able to find a purchase order for the goods received.''

Because this was a standard operating procedure for most manufacturing plants, Deke nodded his understanding as Laurel expected him to.

''When a delivery arrives, we look in there,'' she said, pointing to a gray metal filing cabinet, ''and find the purchase order that matches it. Once we check the packages to be sure they contain the items on the purchase order, we stamp both copies with our Received stamp and send the supplies to Inventory with the pink copy for verification.''

Studying the stamped green copy of the purchase order, Deke again nodded.

''Then we go into the computer, look up the purchase order and mark it in electronically.'' She said this as she continued to sort and stack papers on the table in front of her. ''After everything is recorded in the computer, the green copies are thrown away.'' She nodded in the direction of the papers Deke held. ''Those copies are from items received yesterday. This morning I'll show you how to get into the purchase-order software and mark them Received.'' She caught his gaze. ''Think you can handle that?''

''I can handle that.''

''Good.''

They talked only about work for the rest of the day. When they got home, Laurel started dinner. Deke took Audra to softball practice. Aside from a few giggled comments from Sophie about junior kindergarten, dinner conversation centered on softball. Deke and Laurel's mother cleared up the dishes. Laurel helped with homework. When Deke drove Laurel's mother home for the night, Laurel got the girls ready for bed.

And the whole time Laurel saw—favor by favor,

kindness by kindness—that this man was not at all who he said he was. But more than that, he wasn't who he thought he was. He said he didn't want to be tied down, but he easily committed to Audra and her softball team, he played with Sophie and even drove Judy home. He didn't have a selfish bone in his luscious body.

He also liked company, evidenced by the way he had never used the TV upstairs. He sat downstairs with Laurel, Judy and the girls. He liked being part of a family, and he fit into Laurel's as if he was meant to be there. Yet he honestly believed he wasn't the kind to settle down.

It was all too confusing.

When she went out to the back-porch swing for a few minutes of quiet to try to figure out how a man could talk like a self-absorbed boor and behave like a man ready for the responsibilities of children and a family, she discovered he was already there.

She debated giving him an excuse and not joining him, but because she knew it would be obvious she had changed her mind about coming outside because she didn't want to sit with him, Laurel lowered herself to the creaking wooden swing.

After muffled greetings, Laurel admitted to herself that she was too curious about Deke to have walked away from this opportunity, and she struggled for a way to ask the questions that nagged at her. But sitting so close, she found it hard to remember why she didn't want to be attracted to somebody whose mere presence made her tingly. He wasn't simply a handsome man, he was a good man, and he liked her, too.

Yet they were fighting this.

They were fighting this. Otherwise, he would do more than give her sidelong glances and looks that clearly indicated he found her as attractive as she found him.

In the dewy warmth of the late-spring night, Laurel had a moment of clarity. *They* were fighting this. She wasn't just running from him. He was also running from her. He had his reasons for not wanting to be involved. And the biggest, it seemed, was that he didn't want to get married. He had quickly warned her off.

Silence descended like an ugly blanket, then Deke quietly said, "I have a softball meeting tomorrow night. It's something of an organizational meeting for the coaches, so I can't get out of it."

Laurel laughed. He was apologizing for not being able to be around the following night the way a husband would have. "You're the coach. You're not supposed to try to get out of it."

"Well, it means I won't be able to take your mother home."

"Since you have a genuine commitment, we'll probably even let you out of the dishes," Laurel said with a laugh, then shook her head in wonder. "Something is wrong with you. Something is definitely wrong with you, and I can't put my finger on it."

"Are you going to hang around me until you figure it out?"

"I have to," she said, catching his gaze, trying to communicate that she was looking for a way to minimize the attraction for him as much as for her. All he had to do was cooperate.

"Weren't the things I told you at work enough?"

"You countermand those by how you behave. You see yourself as flighty and irresponsible, but you are one of the most responsible people I've ever met. So you're going to have to give me something better. Something more concrete." Hoping he would allow her this small concession, she met his gaze again.

"Something the girls will believe on our lunch tomorrow."

"How about this?" he said, staring into her eyes, negating every darn word he said with his tormented expression. "Tell them any woman who gets involved with me is only asking for trouble."

"Yeah, right," Laurel said with a laugh. "Like any one of them is going to believe an honest, helpful man like you would be trouble!"

But Deke rose from the swing and started for the kitchen door. When he reached it, he put his hand on the knob as if he would go in without another word, but instead, he faced her again. "Maybe trouble isn't exactly the right word," he said quietly, seriously. "But right now I can't think of a better one to describe my situation, and frankly, even if I could, the full truth isn't something you would want to hear."

With that he walked into the kitchen, letting the wooden screen door close with a soft smack and disappeared into the house.

Dumbfounded, Laurel stared at the bright light shining through the upper half of the closed door.

He had a secret.

Hadn't she realized that all along? A secret easily explained his slim personnel file and the opinion he had of himself that didn't jibe with his real personality.

She wondered if the people at the corporate office knew he was hiding something, then remembered that Tom Baxter had specifically vouched for him. Which meant it had to be a personal secret, not a professional secret.

Unfortunately that only made her all the more curious.

Chapter Four

"Laurel, could you answer a question for me?"

"I'll try," Laurel said, walking over to the computer desk at which Deke sat.

"I know I didn't make a mistake," he said. "I did everything you told me. So, I think something is wrong here."

"Well, show me."

"This purchase order says that there were sixteen screwdrivers ordered."

Reading the green sheet, Laurel nodded.

"But when I go to mark the screwdrivers Received in the computer, not only are they already in, but the purchase order indicates only twelve were ordered."

"Let me see that," Laurel said, pushing Deke over so she could get a better look at the computer screen. As he had said, the items were already marked received, but also as he had said, while the hard copy indicated sixteen were ordered, the computer screen listed only a dozen. "These purchase orders are obvi-

ously stale. Somebody already put them in the system
and forgot to throw them away," Laurel said, not able
to explain the inconsistency and not willing to discuss
it with a trainee. Especially not someone from corporate. If the wrong word got to Tom Baxter, the whole
plant could fall under an investigation for something
that was probably nothing more than a mistake. "So
don't worry about it and just trash them."

"You throw away *all* your hard copies?" Deke
questioned incredulously.

"Well, I throw away *Receiving's* hard copy because
there is no reason for us to keep it. The Purchasing
Department keeps the original purchase order. If everybody kept a copy of everything, there wouldn't be
room to walk in this plant."

"But what if the Purchasing Department doesn't
keep the original?" Deke asked, glancing around oddly
as if he was thinking this situation through and not
liking the conclusion he was drawing.

When Laurel figured out the only conclusion to
which he could be jumping because, with the inconsis-
tencies between the two purchase orders, there was
only one other assumption besides an error, she asked,
"Are you accusing somebody of stealing?"

Deke shook his head. "No," he said, but privately
he realized it was a very good possibility and also an
explanation for why inventory was off. He might have
accidentally stumbled on the answer to the mystery he
had been sent to solve. He still didn't know if this was
a test from his family or a real embezzlement. But because he didn't think Tom Baxter would make a test
so simple, Deke leaned toward believing there really
was a theft scheme of some sort operating here.

But it couldn't be confined to Shipping and Receiving. More than one department would have to be involved, because someone in Shipping couldn't change a purchase order at the stage the product was being ordered, though only someone from Shipping could mark the items Received.

Unfortunately, since he couldn't explain the situation to Laurel or even let her see his interest and alert her to the fact that he was investigating, he had to throw the green copies into the trash and dig them out later. "I'm sure this is some kind of mistake that has a perfectly legitimate explanation."

She smiled at him, watched him throw the green copies into the trash and walked away.

Deke's heart sank. Though he'd tried not to make this connection and he'd also tried to pretend he didn't see the obvious, he had. It was impossible not to.

Because Laurel seemed happy to keep him from looking any farther than he had, if this wasn't a test, if that inventory really was off, if he really was here for the reasons Tom Baxter gave him...

Laurel might actually be a thief.

Laurel didn't know why Deke was quiet and preoccupied at dinner, but she could see it was upsetting Audra.

Not knowing what else to do, she mentioned to her family that Deke had played minor-league baseball, and though Sophie was impressed, Audra almost went into orbit.

"Omigosh!" she yelped.

"It really wasn't that big of a deal," Deke said quietly.

"Not that big of a deal?" Audra echoed, her round brown eyes huge with respect and admiration. "No wonder you can teach us so much!"

"I can teach you so much because you girls are interested and active. You participate. You're willing to work for what you want. My background will have very little to do with your success when you win your division title this summer."

"You think we're going to win?" Audra asked with a happy gasp.

"Don't you?" Deke countered archly.

Audra's eager expression reduced to a sheepish grin. "Yes," she said, then giggled.

"If you don't think you'll win, you won't win," Deke reminded her, and Audra nodded.

The conversation rapidly shifted from Audra's attitude to Sophie and Barbie's Dream House, and soon it was time to clean the kitchen. Deke left for his coaches' meeting with only a quick goodbye. Laurel settled Audra at the kitchen table with her homework, then directed Sophie while she took a bath. She put the girls to bed and only knew Deke was home when she heard him peek into Audra's room to say good-night as had become his practice. She waited for him to come into the living room to watch TV, and when he didn't she assumed he had gone directly to his room.

Though she knew she shouldn't have felt hurt that he hadn't announced himself when he came home, she had. She tiptoed out to the back-porch swing, only to discover that, just like the night before, Deke had had the same idea she had.

Her first instinct was to turn and run. But she couldn't pass up this opportunity to try to figure out why he had suddenly turned cold when he was the one with the secret and *she* was the one who should be cautious. Unless he was angry with her because her poking and prodding into his life had forced him to admit he had a secret. And if that was true and if his secret was personal and not criminal, he had every right in the world to resent her intrusion. Thinking about it that way, she realized she might even owe him an apology.

She ambled over to the swing and said, "Hey."

"Hey," he said, moving over in silent invitation. "Looking for some fresh air, too?"

"Sometimes I need to relax before I can fall asleep."

"I can understand that," Deke said with a chuckle that was the most friendliness and life she had seen out of him in hours. "Your house runs in a sort of organized chaos."

"Doesn't yours?" Laurel asked curiously.

"I'm not home enough to notice," Deke reminded her.

"That's right," Laurel said. Then, before she could stop herself, she asked, "You live with your parents, right?"

"More questions for tomorrow's lunch bunch?" he asked skeptically.

Laurel squirmed. "They'll be brutal."

"I'm sure," Deke shook his head as if annoyed and started to rise from the swing.

Laurel quickly caught his wrist. "I'm sorry. I'm not being honest with you. I'm not asking questions about you for anyone but myself." She raised her eyes until she could look into his. "I can't help it. I'm curious," she whispered, feeling a hundred things she couldn't define or describe when her admission caused something to flare in his beautiful blue eyes. Their gazes met and held.

The current that arced between them was alive with physical awareness and simple human need.

Luckily Sophie saved them. The squeak of the door caught them by surprise, and Laurel dropped Deke's wrist at the same time that he jumped away guiltily. "Is that you, Salami Mommy?"

Deke peered down at Laurel. "Salami Mommy?" he repeated, then pressed his lips into a thin line to keep from laughing.

"Sophie believes very strongly in pet names," Laurel quickly explained to Deke. "And she likes to rhyme."

More loudly to Sophie she said, "Yes, honey, it's me."

"Can I come out, too?"

"No, you need to go back to bed. In fact, I think I'll come in and tuck you in just to make sure it gets done right this time."

"Okay," Sophie said.

Laurel rose from the swing. "Good night," she said, looking at Deke, knowing he was hiding something, and knowing she should be glad he had a secret because it was actually saving both of them.

But she wasn't. Not even a little bit. All she was, was disappointed.

"Have a nice lunch, Laurel," Deke said, lagging behind at his desk, looking as if he was preparing to leave, but not quite ready, though it was already two minutes since the lunch bell had rung. Because it was payday and they had an hour for lunch, instead of just a half hour, all the employees had evacuated as if the cage was on fire. Deke appeared to be in the process of closing out a few things before he left, but his last foot shuffle looked fake. Contrived.

Laurel ambled over to his desk. "I just had a really

good idea. Instead of me fielding questions for you, why don't you have lunch with me and the girls?"

Deke gaped at her. "No way."

"Aw, come on," she said, peeking at the papers on his desk and seeing something that almost took her breath away. "It will be fun."

He shook his head. "Not for me."

"Because you don't want to answer questions?"

He arched an eyebrow. "Would *you?*"

She smiled, trying not to stare at the incriminating evidence on his desk and hoping to temper her own disappointment with cynicism. "I wouldn't hide like a coward."

"I'm not hiding like a coward."

"No," Laurel agreed, reaching for the old purchase-order copies she had told him to trash the day before. "You're actually going to check these out, aren't you?"

He didn't say anything.

Laurel suspected she now knew why he had been so quiet the night before. He had not only disobeyed her, he had every intention of going over her head to Tom Baxter. He might even be starting an investigation that would get some poor soul in trouble for something that was probably nothing more than an honest mistake.

Now she saw the similarities between him and her ex-husband. Now she knew she would have no trouble staying away from him.

"You preppie college kids are all alike," she said, anger in her voice. "You accidentally unearth an error and you want to track down a culprit. Find somebody to blame, look like a hero. Well, get this, Deke. I won't let one of my people go to the gallows because you're trying to make a name for yourself. Somebody made a stupid mistake on a purchase order, probably a typo. It might have even been the procurement officer who wrote the damn thing and not one of my people at all. But you're not the Lone Ranger, or Batman, or even Robin. What you found was a typo. Now go to lunch.''

''Okay, you're right. I'm sorry,'' Deke said as Laurel stormed off.

But she didn't get to the door of the cage before she pivoted to face him again. *He was patronizing her.* She marched back and grabbed the old purchase orders from his hands.

''Don't ever patronize me again.''

Deke watched his evidence, the things he'd found basically by accident ripped from his grasp, and he knew that if he let them go, it might take him months to get this kind of information again. He didn't know if this was a test, but if it was he was about to ace it. If it wasn't, if those books really were off, he might have stumbled on at least part of the theft scheme and he wasn't letting her get away.

He grabbed her wrist and stopped her. ''I wasn't patronizing you. I was trying to do the right thing.''

''And I told you it's probably a typo.''

Deke stared into her eyes. ''What if it isn't?'' he asked quietly.

''If it isn't,'' she angrily deduced, ''it sounds like you're accusing someone of stealing—'' She stopped midsentence and her mouth dropped open. ''My God, you think it's me. You think I'm stealing!''

She threw the purchase orders at him. ''There. There's your evidence. But if you decide to accuse me of stealing, you had better have your facts straight, because if you don't you won't work for this corporation again.''

Deke knew she honestly believed that. She didn't have clout or favors she could call in but genuinely believed she would find a way to get him out. He would have appreciated her confidence, except, in a battle of wills, she didn't stand a chance. Not because he was better or smarter, but because he *did* have clout.

He stood in the empty Shipping and Receiving cage, feeling guilty, feeling awkward and feeling like a criminal again. But he squelched all those emotions and turned on his computer, doing what he was supposed to do. Investigate why that audit was three hundred thousand dollars off. From Laurel's reaction, he no longer believed this was a test. He no longer believed Laurel knew any part of what was going on. He no longer believed his parents or Tom Baxter felt he needed training. He now believed someone was stealing, and unless he was more careful about what he said and to whom, he would blow the carefully constructed cover Tom Baxter had created to help him.

With Laurel furious with him, Deke was glad for softball practice that night. Checking out the old purchase orders Laurel had tossed in his face, he had confirmed what he suspected. The amounts on four of them had been changed. Not enough to call the police, but enough to convince him it wasn't an accident or a typo. He didn't know what his next move should be, but he did recognize that both his stepfather and Tom Baxter expected him to keep his eyes open and his wits about him. Since keeping his wits about him required that he stay loose and comfortable, he was better off not being around Laurel right now.

Besides, the sky was blue. The girls were chipper and having fun. Even a few parents had stopped by to watch the practice. All he had to do was breathe the fresh air and fall headfirst into his passion, and he would get all the relaxation he needed.

Unfortunately Audra reached for an oversize bat, and rather than get his few minutes of peace, Deke had to march over and correct her.

"Not that one," he said, taking the big bat from her hands. "That one."

Shielding her eyes from the sun, Laurel's little brunette with the saucy brown eyes blinked up at him. "I'm trying to increase my bat size by using a bat too big for me. Mr. Marshall used to tell us to do that all the time."

"Well, Mr. Marshall's not here now. I am."

"But he was right! I know he was right. I asked my teacher. She said using a bigger bat would make me stronger."

"All right, fine," Deke said, wondering why he was arguing with an eight-year-old. If she had to learn the lesson the hard way, she had to learn the lesson the hard way. "You're just like your mother," he muttered as he walked away.

But apparently Audra heard him because she said, "You think so?"

Deke stopped and faced the squinting little girl again. For a second he thought he might have insulted her. Instead, sassy, determined Audra appeared inordinately pleased.

"Absolutely," he said, then walked back to the spot from which he could observe both pitcher and batter.

"All right!" Audra said, running to the plate. As she prepared to take her turn at bat, Deke saw her arms shaking under the weight of the heavy instrument.

"You be careful," he called, watching closely. He

would give her a swing or two to prove his point, but
then he was going to take the big bat away. First,
though, he had to make sure she didn't hurt herself.

He easily persuaded her to go back to her normal
bat size after her second swing produced nothing but
air, and he realized, though Audra could be as stubborn
as her mother, time and logic usually got her to see the
light.

He didn't think he would ever get Laurel to see the
light, then wondered what light he was trying to get
her to see. For Pete's sake, he had virtually accused
her of stealing. Not intentionally. Actually, all he had
done was not count her out of the list of suspects, but
he still didn't blame her for being angry with him. If
the tables were turned, *he* would be angry.

Watching her help Audra with homework that night,
Deke went from understanding Laurel's anger to feeling guilty for suspecting her. Laurel was a woman
struggling to support her family. And she was doing an
incredible job. She had provided not a house, but a
home. Complete with a place for Judy, her mother. She
talked with the girls about their little troubles as if they
were of monumental importance because to Sophie and
Audra they were. She cooked, she puttered around
straightening the house at night, she baked special
treats. Simple stuff. Common ordinary things. But
things that made her world and her family's quietly
special.

He wondered how it would feel to have a simple life
like hers. Though her world would be considered hum-
ble by his parents' standards, Deke wasn't so blind that
he didn't see that Laurel was happy. So were her kids.
So was her mother. He didn't think he had ever seen
this much peace in one place, then reminded himself

that the Graham-Bertrim-Smith household had its share of happiness, too. A man who literally had everything he wanted his entire life could not call himself unhappy. He was most certainly happy.

Well, maybe not happy, but he wasn't unhappy. He was a pampered only child who was heir to a fortune. That was not a bad deal to stumble into.

Unfortunately, for some reason, lately he had been wondering if it was the deal he wanted. Not that he didn't want to take over for his stepfather, but it was more that he had never had a choice. No one had asked him if he wanted the job. He had simply been told that Roger would retire in two years and it was time to come home. No one had asked if he wanted to. Even *he* hadn't considered that he didn't want to, because everyone knew he didn't have a choice.

Laurel had choices. Everything she had, she had gotten for herself. And because of that, she had a different kind of experience of life than he did, which resulted in a gut-level certainty that allowed her to say what she wanted when she wanted to say it. She was exactly who she wanted to be.

In some ways he actually envied her. And he didn't want to believe she was a thief. If it killed him, he was going to prove she had nothing to do with this. Deke decided he would question her in order to find the way or reason to take her off his list of suspects.

After the girls were in bed, he peeked out at the back-porch swing and discovered she wasn't there. No big surprise. She probably didn't want to run into him as she had the two previous nights. He walked through the downstairs, checking the dining room, living room and kitchen and not finding her. For a minute he worried that she might be in bed and he wouldn't get to talk to her, but he remembered she had told him about a pool table in the basement and decided to check that out before giving up.

As he hoped, she was there. Alone. Holding a stick, examining the lay of the balls on the table.

"Something I can do for you?" she asked without even looking up.

"No," he said, then took a seat on the steps so he could have a clear view as she shot. "I was just looking for a little company."

"I'm not good company tonight."

"I'm not, either."

"Then maybe it would be wise for us to be away from each other?" she said, still refusing to look at him.

"Come on, Laurel, don't be mad at me."

"I'm not mad at you. You disgust me."

Deke couldn't help it, he laughed. "Well, that makes me feel better."

"I don't care how you feel."

"Isn't that the result you've been after all along?"

She blew her breath out on a long sigh, then sliced the pool stick across the table, forcing three solid-colored balls into the pockets. "Yeah."

"Okay, then. You got what you wanted."

She looked up at him. "So did you. You wanted to dislike me as much as I wanted to dislike you. It appears we both got what we wanted."

"Amen," Deke said, then tilted his head cockily. "The thing is, I'm not sure why you want to dislike me so much. Usually women love me. But from the second day I was here, I knew you were going to use my good looks and charm against me."

His arrogant comment accomplished its goal. All

pretense gone, all anger forgotten, she gaped at him. "No conceit in your family. I can see you have it all."

"It's not conceit if I state a fact to prove a point."

"And what point is that?"

"That you don't like me because of something someone else did. I'm guessing it was your ex-husband."

"Well, you guess right."

A few minutes passed with Laurel resetting the balls on the table after she scratched the eight. When she broke without another word, Deke groaned. "Come on, tell me."

"No, thanks. That's kind of above and beyond the call of duty for your housekeeper, cook and part-time teacher at work."

He heard the way she clearly defined her place in his life. Since he wasn't sure if she'd done that for him or for herself, he ignored it.

"But he hurt you?"

She shrugged. "He left me with two babies and lots of bills. He forced me to get very smart very quickly, and now I have an excellent job in management. I'm a respected, well-liked person at work and in my community." She shrugged again. "In some ways I think he did me a favor."

"Interesting," Deke said, realizing she believed it was true, and also that she didn't harbor any resentment. Unfortunately, being left with two kids and bills made her vulnerable, and the things she was telling him about her life weren't helping to prove her innocence.

But obviously unaware of why he was probing, Laurel looked at him as if he was crazy. "What? You've never met anyone who had to pick up the pieces and go on with the rest of her life or his?"

Knowing he had to stay in the conversation as it fell and could only subtly shift it for his own purposes, Deke recognized he had to answer her question. "No. I've seen guys leave the league, but I never saw what happened after that."

Laurel opened her arms with a smile. "I'm what happens next. This is real life. You look around, consider your options and do the best you can."

"You almost make it sound like fun," Deke suggested.

"It can be," she agreed, but he heard the caution in her voice. "It's all about being flexible and rolling with the punches, or just hanging on when another person would fall apart. I did a little bit of everything. Mostly I just hung on, but I'm not ashamed to admit I grabbed the opportunities that came my way."

He studied the homey finished basement as he thought of the comfort of the rest of her house. She didn't have so much that she couldn't have acquired it on her own with craftiness. But she had enough that a second source of income might have been necessary. "You've done very well."

She glanced around appreciatively. "Yes, I have. But to be honest, Deke, I'm prouder of the girls, of how happy they are and how honest they are, than I am of this house."

Relief washed over Deke when she made that comment, because it didn't sound like the sentiment of a thief. He also understood why she would be pleased with the way her daughters were turning out. Thinking of Audra at softball practice that afternoon, he laughed. "I told Audra today that she was like you and she took it as a compliment."

"Really?" Laurel asked, smiling in spite of herself.

"Yeah." He paused, caught her gaze. "I can see why."

"No, you can't," Laurel scoffed, then resumed her pool game. "We're just little people, living a little life."

"A happy life."

She crashed the cue ball into the three. "Yeah, but we're never going to have the world by the string."

He heard the bitterness in her voice and knew money wasn't a completely resolved issue in her life. Still, watching her walk around the table looking for her next shot, knowing she hadn't had the easiest life in the world, he felt awful for insulting her and wished he could tell her that he could fix it. He wanted to fix it. He wanted being with her to be comfortable again.

As she hit the cue ball into the seven, she added, "Someday you *will* have the world by the string."

"Maybe having the world by the string isn't all that it's cracked up to be."

"Don't say that until you've had a chance to try it," Laurel said with a laugh before she leaned over the table to eye the balls.

Her laugh proved they were on okay ground again, but he couldn't dismiss the obvious. Though she wasn't driven to pursue money for the sake of power and prestige, she did want it. And for the same reason most people wanted it: Money solved problems. Which meant he hadn't cleared her.

But her comment spurred deeper feelings in him and made him think about things in his own life he had been avoiding. He had tried the top and he wasn't sure he liked it. That was the whole reason he felt almost angry about not getting the choice of whether or not he would take over the company.

But he had never had these feelings before and didn't know what caused them now. He could think he was getting them because he was two years away from actually taking the reins of his family's company and suddenly everything was real. Or he could be brutally honest and recognize that it was only when he was around Laurel that he didn't want to be at the top anymore. In her house, on her swing, eating chicken and dumplings, coaching new ball players eager to learn, chatting with parents after softball practice and winding down at the end of the day with someone he was coming to consider a friend, he found he didn't want to live in an ivory tower anymore.

The truth was, he wanted what she had. He wanted real relationships with real people for whom he could do real favors and who would do nice things for him, like bake a pie.

In fact, he felt like a backward Cinderella. And that was the problem. The slipper that wasn't supposed to fit was fitting as if it was made for his foot. He liked it here. He liked Laurel, her family, her life.

The only problem was, he wasn't sure she wasn't a thief.

Chapter Five

By Friday afternoon Deke hadn't found another piece of evidence concerning the suspected theft, and not only was he frustrated, but also he wondered if he hadn't made a mountain out of a molehill because he desperately wanted to look good in his stepfather's eyes.

With Laurel still wary of him, he couldn't ask for help or suggestions, and she sure as hell wasn't volunteering any. Because she was virtually ignoring him, she wasn't even teaching him the basics she was supposed to be teaching him. Not that he blamed her. He had all but called her a suspect in a theft. That would make anyone standoffish.

They both needed some rest and relaxation, and not only would the weekend provide that but also Audra's softball team had its first game early Friday evening. While Deke handled some last-minute coaching preparations, Laurel rushed to make a quick supper.

When his duties were completed, he helped Judy set

the table, and that was when he noticed the check from
the corporate office sitting bigger than life on the cabinet. A woman of no secrets or artifice, Laurel never
thought to hide it or keep it confidential, and when
Deke saw how much she was getting paid to let him
live with her for a week he realized Laurel Hillman
wasn't his thief. She didn't hide things. Her life was
an open book. So she couldn't be the person stealing
from Graham Metals. Period.

As far as he was concerned, her name was cleared.

"Can I help with that?" he asked, taking a dish of
cold cuts from Laurel's hands and giving her a smile.

She peered at him skeptically. "I suppose so, since
you've already got it."

"Right," he said, then started to laugh. He had never
felt that kind of pressure before. He didn't realize how
much he wanted her to be as good, pure and nice as
she seemed until he'd cleared her name. He was giddy
with both gratitude that she wasn't corrupt and the realization that she really was everything he yearned for
her to be. She might be the first truly honest person he
had ever dealt with, if only because she didn't kiss his
butt. Just the thought made him laugh again.

"We'll just chalk this silliness up to your being a
little nervous about the game," Laurel said to Deke as
they sat down to eat their dinner of sandwiches and
soup.

"I'm not!" Audra said. "We're going beat their
socks off."

"Don't get too cocky," Deke said, glad to stop his
giddiness. "Too much confidence can lose a game as
much as no confidence."

"Yes, sir," Audra said, appropriately contrite.

But Deke didn't heed his own warning about over-confidence. He was soaring with it. Laurel Hillman had shown herself to be a good, honest woman and had done so without even trying. She didn't give a damn what he thought about her, and the crazy part was, that made him like her all the more.

Deke and Audra drove to the game an hour early so there would be time to run the girls through the warm-up drills before the spectators arrived. One by one the members of the team jogged onto the field, each of them looking cute and professional in the navy-blue-and-white uniforms. He had decided to get the girls' new suits out of layaway without making the team hold a fund-raiser to earn them because they needed the boost to counteract the retirement of the old coach. Since Deke suspected Tom Baxter might have paid Artie Marshall to take the year off so Deke would have something to do at nights, he also figured he owed these kids.

Wearing the same uniform as the girls, Deke ran them through stretching exercises. As the opposing team warmed up, his girls talked bat weights and strategies, and giggled about getting their first win. But through it all Deke's attention strayed to the stands. Exactly ten minutes before the game he saw Sophie bolt around the fence and to the bottom row of the bleachers. Following a few seconds behind her were Laurel and Judy.

He automatically raised his arm to wave. Looking puzzled, as she had ever since his giddiness at dinner, Laurel cautiously waved back.

Judy grinned and waved. "Go get 'em, girls!" she yelled before she took her seat beside Sophie.

It tickled Deke that Laurel looked confused. Though he found Laurel's unapologetic take-me-as-I-am demeanor sexy in a challenging kind of way, Deke still believed a little payback was in order. He had gone through absolute torment for days, worrying that his actions might put her in jail, and she probably hadn't given him a moment's consideration.

Well, he planned to fix that.

Without thought of consequences, he sprinted over to the spectator section, grabbed the top of the chain-link fence and grinned over it at her. "Hi."

Again she gave him the puzzled look. "Hi."

"Audra tells me we're ready for this season," Judy said, happily jumping in.

"Oh, we're ready, all right," Deke said, but his gaze never released Laurel's. "We finally got all our ducks in order, the training is over, and now we're going to play."

If he hadn't been holding her gaze the entire time he spoke, Laurel would have believed he was talking about softball. Because his eyes held her captive and because those same eyes seemed to darken and become more expressive with every word he said, she knew darned well he wasn't talking about softball.

Heat was generated in her chest and started climbing to her neck and then her face. Apparently seeing her blush of understanding, Deke's grin grew.

"This is going to be some game," he said, laughed heartily, then ran back onto the field.

Laurel collapsed against the bench seat behind her.

"He really loves softball, doesn't he?" Judy said, her gaze following Deke onto the field.

"He seems to," Laurel concurred, but she swallowed. She turned her eyes in the same path as her mother's. But where Laurel was sure Judy saw a nice man with a good heart, giving his all for a bunch of little girls who needed him, Laurel noticed the snug fit of his suit and how absolutely gorgeous he was. She remembered how she had struggled not to thank him for paying to get these uniforms out of layaway from Jeb Pinos, the local sporting-goods supplier, and all kinds of feelings tumbled through her.

He was nice, he was handsome, he wasn't anything like her ex-husband or the other executive trainees who participated in the Graham Metals program—and he liked her. He liked the way she looked. He loved the way she cooked. He appreciated her simple lifestyle. He didn't want her to change, to move, or to pretend to be something she wasn't. He liked her just the way she was. Or at least he had until he found those purchase orders and almost accused her of stealing. It also seemed he had come to terms with their attraction and had decided to do something about it.

From just imagining that he might act on his attraction, heat surged through her again, and she tugged at the neck of her sleeveless sweater.

"It is a little warm this evening, isn't it," Judy said, glancing around.

"Very warm," Laurel agreed, but she was looking at Deke.

Still practicing, one of the members of the opposing team hit a pop fly that flipped over the fence and landed in front of Laurel, bringing her back to reality. Before she could react, let alone reach down to grab the thing and toss it to the pitcher, Deke yelled, "I'll get it."

He ran over and bent down to scoop up the ball. Before he unbent, he peeked up at her, grinned foolishly and said, "Hey." Then he quickly righted himself, tossed the ball and darted off.

Laurel's heart almost burst in her chest. Not only was he flirting with her, but it was in public no less.

She peered at the rows of spectators behind her and realized that at least three quarters of the town was in attendance. Which meant this little escapade of his was taking place in front of everybody.

When she saw her mother's serene, untroubled countenance, she realized she might be panicking for nothing. If her mother, sitting only a foot away, hadn't noticed Deke's odd behavior, then surely no one else had.

She comforted herself with that knowledge and settled down to watch the game as the home team ran onto the field. Because Audra was in the outfield, Laurel didn't expect her to see too much action and she relaxed.

Leaning against the bleacher behind her and shielding her eyes from the sun with her hand, she scanned the scene for her daughter, but before she even caught sight of her, Deke, who was suddenly somehow right beside her, said, "Left field." He caught her arm and pointed it in the direction of Laurel's oldest child.

Though she saw Audra quickly and easily, and though Deke dropped her arm almost as unobtrusively as he grabbed it, the spiral of feeling that radiated from the spot where his hand touched her bare skin resonated through her, and she held back a shiver.

"See her?" Deke asked, smiling.

Laurel cleared her throat. "Yeah, I see her."

"Good," Deke said, turned and went back to the team bench as the umpire yelled, "Play ball!"

He started calling out coachlike things to his players, and Laurel's eyes narrowed in consternation. She had to be imagining there was more behind the things he was saying and doing. Not only did he look totally unaffected, but everything he had said was legitimate and logical. True he was giving her more attention than the average fan, but he lived with her and her daughters. They were more than fans; they were like family to him.

She drew a big breath and focused on the game, convinced she had imagined everything, but when another foul ball looped over the fence and landed too close for comfort, Deke was standing in front of her in seconds.

"That might not be the safest place to sit," he said.

Judy said, "Amen," and started climbing a little higher on the bleacher.

But Laurel only stared up at Deke because he was staring down at her. Smiling. She could handle the smile. But it was the darned gleam in his eyes that was getting to her. She couldn't imagine how a person could make his face look concerned while sending a completely different message with his eyes. But that was exactly what he was doing. Anyone who saw him would think he was a diligent official, trying to make sure fans didn't get hurt. But in his eyes were the sparks, the heat and the unspoken hint that for some reason everything between them had changed and he had picked this very public arena to tell her.

Knowing she had to break the contact, she rose, intending to climb up a few rows to get out of the way of trouble. But Deke didn't step back, and when she stood, they were so close they almost brushed.

"I'd go up to about row five," he said, his warm breath fanning her face.

Laurel stood before him dumbfounded. For a good ten seconds she could have sworn he was about to kiss her. He glanced at her mouth and seemed to pause in his breathing. Laurel knew her heart stopped. Stopped. Just plain stopped. Like her breathing and the game and the rest of the world.

But rather than kiss her, he lifted his gaze back to hers and whispered, "Go to at least row five and you won't get hurt."

Staring into his beautiful blue eyes, Laurel knew for certain that wasn't true. If she followed up on all the promises and hints in those gorgeous eyes, she would most definitely get hurt.

"Row five," she repeated, then swallowed hard.

The rest of the game passed in a blur for Laurel. Though she tried to see every good play made by her daughter, every hit and even every good reason Audra had missed a play or a hit, she couldn't stop thinking about Deke.

Deke had never had so much fun in his life. Laurel was teaching him far more about life than she ever would about shipping and receiving. Frankly he didn't care as much about shipping and receiving as he cared about the new feelings she inspired in him and the new world she seemed to be opening up to him. As a minor-league baseball player he had mixed and mingled with fans and supporters for PR, but though the fans shared his enthusiasm for the game, they hadn't shared their lives or their emotions as easily as Laurel did. Everything she thought and felt was right there in her eyes for him to read, and Deke felt himself truly communicating with another person for the first time in his life.

It was so good and so honest and so darned right that he didn't stop to think about consequences.

"How about ice cream to celebrate our win?" he

asked when the other team members had gone and he and Audra were done piling equipment into his car.

"Oh, you guys go on ahead," Judy said, batting a hand in dismissal. "I'm exhausted. I haven't shouted that much in years. Mrs. Oldham will give me a ride home." She turned and started walking away, waving and yelling, "Hey, Ginny, wait up!"

"I guess it's just you and me and the girls, then," he said to Laurel. When she blushed, Deke smiled. "Has anyone ever told you you're very readable?"

"Of course," Laurel said, sounding exasperated. "Why do you think I don't say much?"

"Probably because you don't have to," Deke said, then laughed. "Come on. Everybody hop in my car. We'll get some ice cream, relax for a minute and go home."

"All right," Audra said, opening the back door automatically as she realized her front-seat spot would be usurped by her mother. Sophie climbed in behind her older sister.

"Seat belts," Laurel said, then reluctantly took the door handle of the front-seat passenger's side.

Deke beamed with pride. Again, he was fitting into her world as if he belonged there. It made him feel proud and strong and something like a male lion to have Laurel and the girls all to himself. He didn't even mind that he had to wait twenty minutes to get served because every other parent had the same idea about ice cream he had.

When he walked away from the windmill that served as the business establishment to the picnic table where the family sat, Deke handed a vanilla cone to Sophie, chocolate to Audra and her mother, and kept a vanilla cone for himself. He felt as if he was experiencing life—the kind of life normal men experience—for the first time.

Everything in this silly little town was real and wonderful. He'd had a few spats with the girls on the team. He had even argued with two of the parents. But rather than get angry or frustrated, he had the sense that real life required a few disagreements to set the world on the proper axis. He appreciated that none of these people knew who he was. He liked being judged only on the merits of his abilities. And he liked Laurel, her daughters and her peaceful unpretentious home.

"I love chocolate," Audra said with a sigh, then licked her ice cream again.

"I love chocolate, too," Laurel said every bit as dreamily, and Deke laughed.

"You'd swear it was in scarce supply the way you women moon over it," he said as Sophie walked along the bench seat toward him.

She held her ice cream in one hand and wrapped the other around his neck. His arm immediately went to her tiny waist to ensure she didn't fall.

"Yeah, the way you women moon over it," she parroted, obviously taking Deke's side in the argument.

He tickled her belly. "What are you talking about? You're a woman, too."

"I am not!" She giggled. "I'm just a kid."

"A cute kid," Deke said, enjoying her.

She giggled again. "A cute kid," she agreed, wrapping her other arm around his neck to hug him.

Even as she said the words, something cold and wet dripped down the back of his neck. Knowing her ice cream was in the hand she just put around him, Deke held back a shriek. Because she was only four, Sophie wouldn't be smart enough to realize that her cone might leak.

"Sophie, honey," he said sweetly, "you really shouldn't be holding ice cream when you hug somebody."

"Oh, no!" Laurel cried, jumping up.

"It's okay," Deke said. "She dripped a few drops, that's all. I won't die."

With that he settled Sophie on his lap, recognizing that she relished his attention and also that he didn't mind having hers. Laurel sat down again to finish her ice cream, but Audra asked to be excused to visit with some friends.

"Okay," Laurel said, "but not for long. I'm tired and want to go home."

"Oh, I'm sorry," Deke said immediately. "I didn't realize you were tired. We can go now if you want."

"No, no," Laurel said lightly. She didn't appear nervous anymore, but relaxed and comfortable, as if she had forgotten all his flirting.

Deke pondered for a moment that in his old world he might have been insulted by that, but realized that in this world sexual tension and flirting were more private things. He also knew that because they were more private things, they were more special. He would wait until they were alone before he flirted with her again, and it would be fun, secret and only theirs. He felt a thrill just thinking about it.

Seeing Laurel's face flush, he realized he was staring at her and he pulled his attention away. He was a patient man. He could wait until they got home and, in waiting, make everything that much sweeter.

He tickled Sophie's tummy again. "Done with that cone yet?"

Turning her ice-cream-covered face up to him, she grinned. "No."

"Well, you better hurry, because if you don't, it will melt all over you."

"And you," Laurel observed wryly.

"That's okay. I don't mind."

A silence descended over them. The air of the late-May night was beginning to cool as darkness fell. Deke observed it all like a man who had never seen dusk before. He had the sudden and intense feeling that he had never lived before, and seriously wondered if that wasn't what attracted him to this town and this woman.

"Are you going to marry my mommy?"

Jolted out of his reverie, Deke stared at Sophie. "What?"

"Are you going to marry my mommy?"

"Sophia Maria!" Laurel gasped.

The quiet night seemed to get even quieter. Laurel was embarrassed, but also seemed accepting of the fact that four-year-olds said things without realizing what they were saying.

But the truth was the truth. And Deke also realized that in a way his actions were leading them down the very path Sophie suggested. He was flirting with Laurel, flirting with her life and her lifestyle, falling in love with her town. Backhandedly making commitments. Promises. Hinting they might have a future together.

And it might not be because this was what he wanted, but because he didn't want the life to which he was destined. He couldn't be so foolish as to ignore the possibility that all this might be tempting because his other life was suddenly beginning to feel like a prison. And to escape that prison, albeit temporarily, he was playing the role of husband so that Laurel would go along with him.

Sitting at the picnic table, staring at ingenuous Sophie, who had forced everybody back to reality, Deke was shamed by the knowledge that in his own short-sighted quest he hadn't given a thought to the fact that he might inadvertently hurt Laurel. And Sophie. And Audra.

Hoisting Sophie off his lap, Laurel called, "Let's go. Audra. We're ready now."

Deke rose. He had been having so much fun that he'd forgotten the realities of his life. He couldn't make a commitment to Laurel's family. Hell, even if she were childless, he couldn't say with certainty that he could make a commitment to Laurel. He had enough commitments. He couldn't make another.

But more than that, he had to be honest and admit he might not be as attracted to Laurel and her life as he was disenchanted with his own life. Maybe all this looked so good because it wasn't an existence that was being forced down his throat.

"Want some company?"

Deke glanced over at the open screen door to see Laurel as she stepped out onto the back porch.

"Yeah. Sure."

She made her way to the swing quietly. When she sat next to him, she said, "Look, I'm sorry. I'm not going to make any excuses for Sophie's saying what she'd said. She's four. To her, the world is black and white."

Deke looked down at his feet. He wasn't so much baffled by what Sophie had said as his own stupidity for not realizing it was coming. "That's okay."

For several seconds Laurel didn't say anything, and by the time Deke realized she was waiting for him to look at her, she appeared to be furious. And he understood why. He had gone from flirting with her to not saying anything and his quiet appeared to have been inspired by her daughter's comment. If she was angry, it was because she felt he was put off by her child.

"What is that supposed to mean? Sophie is a little girl. She asked a question that was obvious to her. You don't have to act like somebody tried to shoot you."

"I'm not acting like—"

"Don't give me that!"

"Look, you don't know—"

"I know a heck of a lot more than you think I do!" she said, jumping from the porch swing and glaring down at him. "You're some hotshot from the corporate office who comes to our little plant in Maryland thinking he's better than everybody else. Well, guess what? You aren't."

"I never said—"

"You didn't have to say anything," Laurel told him angrily. "Your actions speak a lot louder than words! As if we'd want anything to do with you," she muttered, pacing to the porch wall. "Take a look around you, Mr. Bertrim. We're not that desperate."

Deke was off the swing and behind her before she had a chance to make the turn in her pacing. When she did pivot around, she almost bumped into his chest.

"Neither am I."

"Really?" she scoffed, accepting his unspoken challenge by refusing to back away from him or release his gaze. "I've never seen anybody who jumped at the chance to help with dishes, volunteered to coach a little girls' softball team and even paid for the uniforms himself. If that's not desperate—''

He grabbed her upper arms, yanked her up and kissed her soundly on the mouth before she said anything else. But though it had been his intention to shut her up, the feeling of her mouth under his not only obliterated his thought processes, it turned on about thirty-six instincts Deke was holding back only by sheer force of will.

His blood heated, all his nerve endings came to life, his libido yawned and stretched and woke up as if from a long winter's nap. Forgetting everything but the taste and feel and scent of her, he stopped the angry onslaught of his lips and slowed the pace, tentatively rubbing his mouth across hers, as if experimenting with the feeling. When she moaned, echoing the emotions ricocheting inside him, he pressed his mouth a little harder, tasting her, feeling her, wondering how he'd ever gone thirty-three years without experiencing all the wonderful things bubbling inside him.

Then he remembered. He was heir to a throne, of sorts. He had a business to run, a family fortune to guard and grow. He might get a wife and family, but that would probably be somewhere down the road. And that wife and family would not throw him into uncomfortable positions or shoot feelings and sensations through him that would make him forget who he was and what he should be doing.

He pulled his mouth away, then took a step back.

Laurel only stared at him.

He swallowed. ''Sorry.''

Holding his gaze, as though trying to figure out if he pulled away because he didn't think she would make a suitable wife, Laurel lifted her chin and said, "I'll bet you are."

"Not for the reasons you think."

She smiled wearily. "Yeah. I'm sure."

"Laurel, I have a lot of stuff I have to do with my life."

She nodded. "Me, too."

"I mean it," he said, then rubbed his hand across the back of his neck. "You really don't want to get involved with me if you can help it."

With that he turned and strode to the screen door and into the kitchen without so much as a backward glance.

Laurel stared at the door. Her lips tingled. Her limbs ached from the effort not to melt against him as he kissed her. He might be warning her off, which was the kind and gentlemanly thing to do, but if the way he kissed her was any indicator, he hadn't wanted to.

She debated going into the house, finding him and kissing him again, just to test his control, because their chemistry was so strong it was almost a shame to waste it. Then she remembered he had a secret and she didn't get involved with upwardly mobile trainees. She didn't belong in their world, and they were only passing through hers.

How was it that Deke had managed to get her to forget that?

Chapter Six

Monday afternoon Laurel walked past Deke's desk, and he pretended to be occupied with some papers by his keyboard. Unfortunately he knew she recognized that he wasn't really working on the stack of purchase orders, but trying to access software that was off-limits when she asked, "What are you doing?"

With a quick flick of his hand on the mouse, he minimized the image on the screen and said, "Just browsing."

"You were in the accounting software."

He turned and gave her a bland look. "I'm a trainee. I'm trying to learn everything I can."

"But you're not supposed to be able to get into that."

He shrugged. "I couldn't. I got as far as the opening menu, but that was it."

She said, "Thank heaven for small blessings," but wouldn't stop staring at him suspiciously.

Deke became incredibly uncomfortable. He thought

it was safe to try to get a peek at some of the software besides the series of windows and menus used for shipping and receiving, because the employees were on a fifteen-minute break. Even Laurel had been gone. But just when he got involved in the software and stopped watching his back, she'd suddenly appeared behind him.

"You're not going to report me to somebody, are you?"

"Why not? You were ready to accuse me of stealing."

"I never really thought you were the person doing the stealing."

"Oh, so you're still convinced there's a thief because a few purchase-order copies didn't get thrown away."

"No, I'm convinced there's a thief because the numbers were changed."

"On one purchase order."

"On four out of fifteen."

Hearing that, Laurel collapsed on the edge of his desk. "That's a little too many to be a coincidence."

Because Deke had already cleared Laurel to his own satisfaction and because he was getting nowhere fast investigating on his own, he made the quick but certain decision to seek her help. Unfortunately that meant he had to be honest with her—about everything.

"There are a lot of things happening at this plant that seem like a coincidence but aren't."

Her eyes narrowed and she crossed her arms on her chest. "I'm listening."

"For one, I'm not really an executive trainee. I'm here because the last corporate audit for this plant revealed a discrepancy of almost three hundred thousand dollars.''

"What!''

Her genuine surprise fortified Deke's belief that he could trust her. "Yeah. But that's not the worst of it.'' He paused and caught Laurel's gaze. "I'm Roger Smith's stepson. Mimi *Graham* Smith is my mother. My father, Paul Bertrim, died when I was thirteen. Roger was hired to run the conglomerate temporarily. He and my mother fell in love, and I got a two-decade reprieve from taking over the business, but I'm the next person in line to be CEO of Graham Industries.''

If she hadn't already been sitting, Laurel knew she would have collapsed. "You have to be kidding.''

"Afraid not.''

"Great. Just great,'' she said, squeezing her eyes shut with misery. Her daughter had insulted him. She'd kissed him. She was unbearably attracted to him and frequently couldn't hide it—and he owned the company for which she worked. She couldn't even yell at him for deceiving her or bring him to task. He controlled her raises, her promotions...her life as long as she worked here.

She wished the earth would open up and swallow her.

"At first I thought all this might have been a setup. Something like a test for me to prove that I'll be able to take over when my stepfather retires two years from now. Even finding those stale purchase orders like I did seemed too easy. But since there haven't been any other clues in over two weeks, I'm not so sure anymore.''

Ignoring her misery, Laurel stayed focused on the problem at hand, because if she didn't, she knew she would say something she'd regret. If she had known who he was, she would have treated him very differently and she wouldn't have been embarrassed right now. But she didn't even have the luxury of confronting him about keeping his identity a secret. If he had come here announcing with a blare of trumpets that he was looking for a thief, that person would have disappeared. Still, she wasn't convinced that there was a thief.

"If this was a test, I doubt that your stepfather or Tom Baxter would make it easy."

Deke grinned and all Laurel's feminine yearnings surged to the forefront. He was so handsome and so sexy and so physically perfect that she'd had the devil's time fighting this attraction. But now she knew why all her warning signals wouldn't let her fall victim to his good looks and potent charm. He wasn't simply on the fast track like her ex-husband. Someday he would be at the very top.

Heck, he *was* the top!

"If my mother had anything to do with it, they would."

"Well, maybe your mother didn't," Laurel said, standing and stepping away from his desk. Away from him. This was it. The end. If she hadn't been convinced to keep her distance before this, she was certainly convinced now. After all the odd things they had been through because of living together, she wasn't even sure she could salvage her reputation. And forget about her pride—that was long gone. She had *kissed* him. She had kissed the man who owned the company! And he knew she wanted to kiss him again, because after the kiss, he had warned her that she shouldn't get involved with him. Now she knew why.

"Unless you have something more solid to go on than a few easily discovered purchase orders, I don't think you should jump to conclusions."

Deke caught her hand when she went to turn away. "I didn't come here to make a mess out of things, but I would like to pass this test, if that's what it is."

"So what do you want from me?" Laurel asked, angry that he couldn't just let her go, because with every second that ticked off the clock she became more miserable. In spite of the fact that he had warned her off, in spite of the fact that she had her own internal warnings, in her heart she had wished they were on the brink of a relationship. But he was only here to play detective for his family and didn't want anything to do with her. She couldn't say that he led her on. The pain of that even superseded the tingles that resonated through her from his touch.

"Help. Any kind of help you can give me would not only solve my problem, but also it would get me out of here more quickly."

Laurel couldn't stop herself. She smiled grimly. "You're that anxious to get away from us?"

"No," he said. Catching her gaze again, he stared into her eyes, and Laurel felt a hundred things she wished she didn't. Though any longings and yearnings she had for him should have died a quick death with his admission of who he was, they poured through her, instead, and she couldn't look away.

"I'd like nothing better than to stay here forever, but we both know I can't. We both know it's not right."

She did. When common sense and sanity and reason reigned, she knew that their attraction was an aberration of some sort, and she knew it would be wrong to pursue it. She also knew he felt he had no choice but to hide his identity, and she couldn't fault him for doing what he perceived to be his job.

"I'll help you," she said, and walked away as the other employees returned from the cafeteria. Every minute she spent with him made her like him more, and though she knew it was a mistake, she couldn't stop her feelings. It was a toss-up whether he would break her heart because he couldn't take her to the top with him, or he would break her heart because he was afraid of a commitment—evidenced by the way he panicked when Sophie mentioned marriage—but one thing was certain. She knew he would break her heart.

And the sooner she got him out of her life the better.

The next softball game was not peppered with flirting, innuendo and almost kisses. Though Laurel had to admit she missed being the object of Deke's attention, she was also grateful because she recognized what she had to do. Her first goal was to prove to him that those purchase orders he had found were, indeed, part of some kind of test his stepfather and Tom Baxter had organized. Her second goal was to prove to herself that her ironclad control had not been destroyed just because he was a little nicer than her other boarders and a little better-looking.

She planned to accomplish both her goals within the next seven days.

"All right, let's play ball!"

As the umpire shouted the command, Audra's team began to run onto the field, and Laurel waved at her daughter. The game looked and felt exactly like every game from the year before. Except now Deke was the coach, and as he stood on the sidelines calling out instructions and encouragement he was sharp and commanding. Sexy in the way only a naturally born leader can be.

So when she found herself sneaking peeks at him, Laurel told herself not to worry. Not only was he hard to ignore, but the quick glances were something like weaning herself from her growing feelings, and she didn't let herself be concerned about the way her eyes strayed from the field and to the coach more than they should have.

Inning one rolled into inning two, which quickly became inning three. Audra's team had a comfortable three-run lead, and they added another two runs at the bottom of the third. Then suddenly Evie Brown couldn't seem to control her pitching and everything fell apart. Including the mood of the parents in the stands. Laurel didn't like it when their words of encouragement turned into criticism.

A foul ball landed in front of the bleachers, and Deke ambled over to get it. He smiled at the rows of parents. "Relax. We'll come back next inning."

"We better," one of the fathers grumbled, but Deke only nodded and walked away.

If Laurel thought it rattled her when the parents shouted criticisms at the kids, she discovered it shook her even more when they switched the object of their criticism from the players to the coach. As if his appearance in front of the bleachers had made him fair game, Deke quickly became the reason for the bad playing, the bad pitching and even the other team's good luck.

Not quite sure what else to do, Laurel turned to the people who were her friends and neighbors and coworkers and said, "Don't worry. If Deke says we'll come back, we'll come back."

"You got a lotta faith in that guy."

Laurel shrugged. She wondered what Loretta Evans would be saying right now if she knew the "guy" she referred to would someday be running the company for which Loretta's husband worked. "He knows what he's doing. He played minor-league ball."

"He did?" someone asked with enthusiasm.

Laurel nodded. "Yeah, he did. I think we were really lucky to get him."

That seemed to put everybody in a good mood until Audra's team didn't come back at the bottom of the next inning as he had promised. Unfortunately, because Laurel had given such a nice pep talk about Deke, the parental criticism again shifted to the girls.

"Why are they taking this so seriously?" Laurel whispered to her mother.

"Because everybody's tired from having worked all day," Judy said, trying to hush her daughter. "You know these are nice people," she said. "It's just the stress of the moment. Hey, Ump, are you blind? That was a strike!"

Seeing that her mother was as caught up in the game as everybody else, Laurel nervously settled back on her bench seat. Everybody seemed to have higher expectations this year. She suddenly realized she hadn't helped things by bragging about Deke's qualifications. If anything, she might have inadvertently put more pressure on the girls.

"Oh, for Pete's sake, Audra," someone yelled from behind Laurel. "You should have had that!"

Laurel's eyes grew large and round and she pivoted to see who had yelled, but everybody's faces wore the same angry scowl, as the runner from second scored because Laurel's baby girl had missed a fly ball.

"Great, just great!"

Laurel took a deep breath and decided not to add to the mess by defending her daughter—even though she did think it was idiotic to get so carried away. But as the score was being tallied and the teams were getting ready for the next pitch, Laurel saw Audra signal to Deke for time-out. Deke immediately signaled the umpire and Audra began to sprint off the field.

Not only was her daughter holding her hand, but the closer she got, the more suspicious Laurel became that Audra was crying.

"Oh, for heaven's sake, shake it off, Audra!"

"Shake it off!" Laurel said, spinning around to face the crowd behind her again. "She's a child and she's hurt."

"Then maybe she shouldn't be playing ball."

"And maybe you take all this a little too seriously!"

Laurel watched as Deke examined Audra's hand and then directed her to sit on the bench and sent in a replacement. Before Laurel could get up and see for herself what had happened, Deke came over.

"I think she stoved her finger," he said. "If you don't mind, I would like to keep her out for the rest of the game."

"Of course I don't mind."

"You know if she can't take it, maybe she shouldn't be playing," came a comment from the stands.

Laurel watched Deke's expression go from impassive to furious in about a second. "Look, bud," he said, directing his comment to Jimmy Hanson, "the kid is eight. The ball slammed into her hand pretty hard. Could we cut her a break?"

"I say we cut her a permanent break and let her out of the rest of the games."

Obviously not wanting to get into an argument, Deke shook his head and started to walk away, but Nora Reynolds bounced up from her seat. "Why isn't my daughter in?"

Deke stopped, turned around. "Your daughter missed two practices."

"Yeah, but I'll bet if she were Laurel's daughter, she would be in."

"Laurel's daughter didn't miss any practices...but that doesn't matter. I'm the coach. What I say goes. If you don't like that, you can—"

"Fire you?" Norma asked archly.

Suddenly Deke grinned, and though the crowd was oblivious to the absolute stupidity of what Nora Reynolds had said, Laurel saw the humor Deke saw and stifled a giggle.

"No, find another team. I'm here to stay, lady. You can either like it or leave."

With that he turned to walk to the team bench, but appearing to have changed his mind, he came back to the bleachers. "You don't help eight-year-old girls by yelling at them. If anything, you're making things worse. You're also making me see that you people care more about winning than you care about your kids."

He returned to the team bench and signaled the umpire to start the game again. Laurel pressed her lips together to keep from smiling. These people had no way of knowing Deke held their future in his hands. But he never once mentioned that. He kept the argument about exactly what it should have been about as he delivered an appropriate reprimand.

She was as proud of him as she would be if he was her best friend or her husband, and she realized she had much deeper feelings for him than just the silly attraction she thought she was battling. Deke Bertrim was a decent guy who defended little girls and was trying to impress his mother and stepfather. Anybody else might have been insulted that his family wanted to test him, but Deke took it in stride. It was all part of the deal.

Her eyes unexpectedly misted. After some of the things he had told her and the way he sometimes seemed lost and alone, she wondered if he had stood up for the girls, defended them, because no one had ever stood up for him or defended him.

"So why do you think your parents want to test you?"

Laurel had gotten two hours of overtime authorized for both herself and Deke, and they were currently doing the unauthorized work of jumping from one computer program to another, seeing what they could get into without a password. The way Laurel had it figured, they could significantly reduce suspects of who could have done what by seeing what kind of access normal people had to the system. And which people had enough access to change the numbers on a purchase order.

"I don't think my parents want me to be tested. I think it's Tom Baxter."

Laurel burst out laughing. "Tom Baxter? Why?"

"Because he's second in command. Because he'll be answering to me in two years, instead of giving me orders."

"You think he's getting his digs in now?"

"No. I think he's making sure I'm capable of doing the job so he doesn't have to baby-sit me, second-guess my every move or spend the rest of his career worrying."

"That's interesting," Laurel said, watching him flip from one computer screen to the next like changing channels on television, and making notes of what he could get into and what he could do once he got there.

"It's not interesting at all. It's just part of the deal."

"What else is part of the deal?" Laurel asked, unable to help herself. "It seems like you should have a fascinating life."

"I don't," Deke assured her. "I've spent most of my life waiting in the wings."

"That's why you played baseball."

"That and the fact that I love it." He paused as he scrolled down a page, then quietly said, "I miss it."

"Then maybe what you should have done was stay in baseball."

"I wasn't going anywhere…and I'm destined to do this." He paused, caught her gaze. "I know in America we don't value loyalty the way we used to. Most of us hate being told what to do. But my case is very different from most. This is my heritage. This is also my family's fortune. It's something like an honor to be asked to take over."

Laurel shrugged. "I guess…if it's what you want."

"It is," he said, but Laurel noted a distinct lack of enthusiasm in his voice.

"You're sure."

"I'm sure."

"Whatever."

"Whatever," Deke mimicked, then he sighed. "Look, it's not like I'm being sent to prison."

"In a way I think you are."

"Well, you're wrong. I love the idea of being in charge of everything."

"But…" Laurel prodded when he felt silent.

"Some days I'm just not so sure I can do it."

"Why not?"

"Well, given that Tom doesn't have any confidence in me, I lost some of mine."

"I can understand that."

"And, too, I haven't been around as much as someone like Tom, who sits by my stepdad at every meeting. Sometimes I think my family would be smarter to give the reins to him."

Laurel felt a tingle of hope in her chest. If he refused to take over the company, he could stay with her. He could be the funny, warm wonderful person he seemed to want to be. He could kiss her all he wanted. She could kiss him back. "Maybe you should suggest that."

He shook his head. "No, this is what my family wants, so it's my duty to become every bit as good at it as my stepfather. I don't want any other options."

But he did, Laurel realized. He truly did. He missed baseball. He enjoyed helping with dishes. He enjoyed coaching eight-year-old girls, and even handled their parents like a pro. And once he couldn't resist kissing her.

Not only could she think of a hundred reasons he would want more options than the one he had, she could also think of a hundred reasons she would want him to consider other options.

Another little piece of hope sneaked into her heart. He was so different from her ex-husband that if she did allow herself to fall in love with him, he wouldn't desert her. They would make decisions together. They would work together for the common good of their marriage. He would be loyal.

She quickly stopped those thoughts. Blocked them

because they were pure fantasy. There were no guarantees with a man like him, and she wasn't taking any more risks with her heart.

"Well, that's it for me here," Deke said, rising. "I'm going."

"You're leaving?" Laurel was absolutely certain she'd stopped breathing.

"Nope, I'm not leaving. I'm stuck. I can't get into any of the programs. They're airtight and I'm not much of a hacker."

Laurel breathed a sigh of relief until he added, "It's time to go at this from another angle. If this is a test, someone at this plant set things up for my stepfather. Let's look at the personnel files to see who has a reason to get involved or a connection to Tom I don't know about. I'll call my administrative assistant at corporate and see if I can't get some information from her."

"What kind of information?"

"The usual stuff," Deke said, preoccupied with preparing to leave. "Don't worry about it. At my level, my staff and I are authorized to go into anyone's personnel file. I can get anything I need."

That was exactly what Laurel was afraid of, and the one thing she had somehow forgotten when she started weaving forever fantasies about her and Deke. Even if he stayed at Graham Metals, there were things in her past that would make him see he could never make a commitment to her. With his reputation always on the line, he couldn't wish away or ignore the skeletons in her closet. So even if he did fall in love with her, she wouldn't make a good wife for him.

She told herself she didn't care. Leading their two-car parade home that night, she told herself that it shouldn't matter to her that Deke had access to everyone's personnel file and that if he requested information about her, he wouldn't like what he saw. He might be loyal, he might even think he was falling in love with her, but once he discovered the truth about her past, no matter how much he told himself it didn't matter, it would matter. In his world it would matter. So even if he pursued her to high heaven, she would resist him. Which meant it shouldn't matter if he discovered things about her past. She didn't care what he thought of her.

"You can go ahead upstairs and wash up," Laurel suggested airily as she breezed into the kitchen before him. "I'll see what I can find for dinner."

Deke's foot stopped midway up the first step of the kitchen stairs. "Oh, I thought I would take you out. Since your mother has the kids and all, I thought we would... Never mind." He shook his head. "Dumb idea."

"Actually, no," Laurel said, taken aback by his unexpected thoughtfulness. She had no intention of saying that out loud, but once she had, she knew she had to explain. "It was kind of sweet."

Deke rubbed his hand across the back of his neck. "You seem to bring the sweet out in me. I don't act like this around other women." He paused and caught her gaze. "I mean, I do, but it's more a matter of politeness. With you, it's automatic. Almost like I was made to please you."

Laurel's eyes widened. "Stop that. I'll never be able to resist you if you don't stop saying such sweet things."

"Sweet isn't all you bring out in me," Deke warned quietly. "I have a whole range of feelings for you and about you," he said, walking away from the stairs and over to her. "At home, I usually felt very specific things for the women I dated. Some women I was attracted to. Others I liked as friends. But my feelings for you encompass both those things and more." He traced his finger along the line of her cheekbone, sending shivers of awareness through her.

"Part of me wants to take care of you. Part of me wants to lean on you for support. Part of me wants to enjoy your friendship, to play pool and keep the parents at the softball games in line together. But the biggest part of me wants to hug you and kiss you. I like the way you feel. I like the way you smell. Just looking at you sometimes takes my breath away."

He kissed her then, because Laurel realized a man couldn't say those wonderful things to a woman and not kiss her. And while he pressed his mouth to hers, physically expressing the things he had verbalized, she realized she felt the very same way about him. Instinctively she knew she could lean on him even as he depended on her because they'd be partners. He'd share his burdens because they would be equals. In a way, he had always treated her like someone he respected and trusted. Hadn't he ultimately divulged his secret? And hadn't that secret brought them to the level of intimacy they had now?

She loved knowing who he was and not sharing that information with anyone. But most of all, she loved the way he made her feel. Warm and soft. Sexual and hungry. All the things he felt, but in the way a woman experienced them.

He was right. They weren't just attracted to each other, and they weren't meant to be only friends. If they followed up on this attraction, they would want to be everything to each other. But they couldn't. Not as long as his life was so unsettled—or, more to the point, not as long as he believed he had to go home. Then there was the matter of her past. A man like him couldn't marry a woman like her. A commoner. A woman with a past.

Just as she came to this conclusion, Deke pulled back. He studied her for a few seconds, then simply turned away. She didn't need to voice the conclusion she had drawn. He undoubtedly read it in her expression.

So he left her alone in the kitchen.

And Laurel stood, despondent. There was no help for it. She had fallen in love with this man, and tomorrow he would call the corporate office to get background information.

In a few days he would know everything there was to know about her, and then he would run like the devil away from her.

Chapter Seven

In the kitchen the next morning, trying to walk to the refrigerator to get cream for his coffee, Deke bumped into Laurel. Judy was barking orders to the girls about breakfast as Laurel packed brown-bag lunches, so when the collision occurred, it went unnoticed by everyone except Deke and Laurel. Putting his hands on her shoulders to keep her steady, he looked into her eyes, and the entire room, every sound, every person disappeared, except for Laurel.

"Sorry," he said.

She cleared her throat. "That's okay," she said, shifting until she was out from under his hold. She turned away quickly, opened the refrigerator to grab the supplies she needed and nearly ran to the butcher block where she was assembling the lunches.

Deke felt as if somebody had slapped him. He knew they couldn't pursue a relationship, but he thought they were on the same wavelength about regretting it. He couldn't believe he'd misinterpreted her feelings.

"You want to ride to the plant together?" he asked cheerfully, pretending he had imagined her cool reaction.

She shook her head. "No. I have some errands to run at lunch time and I need my car."

"We could take your car..."

She caught his gaze and said, "I want to go in alone."

That he knew he hadn't imagined.

Driving to the factory and even for the first few hours of work that morning, Deke didn't have to wonder about her odd behavior. He'd overstepped a hundred boundary lines when he'd said those things the night before and then kissed her.

But the truth was, like it or not, they weren't simply two people who had accidentally met. The chemistry between them was too powerful to believe that this was a chance meeting, and knowing her was starting to feel as much like his destiny as taking over Graham Industries. Alone in his bed, still tingling and aroused from a simple kiss and bombarded with the intuition that she was meant to be in his life, he decided he didn't want to miss what was happening between them. He wanted to try to figure out what it meant.

She obviously did not.

"Deke?"

Deke turned to see Laurel standing behind him. The bell announcing the first break of the morning began to ring, and everybody from the Shipping and Receiving Department dropped what they were doing and zoomed out of the cage as if every cupcake would be gone if they didn't get to the lunch room immediately.

"Yeah?" Deke said carefully.

"I've been thinking."

He nodded. "So have I."

Deke watched the expression on her face as she recognized the innuendo in his voice, but nonetheless disregarded it before she said, "There has to be a way we can speed up your investigation. There's got to be something we're missing. An angle we're not thinking of—something that would take us to the next step."

He didn't bother reminding her that he had thought of the angle to proceed with when he'd e-mailed his assistant for background information about the plant and its workers, because he knew what she was really telling him. Just as he had thought this over and decided they should examine what was happening between them, she had also done some deliberating, decided against exploring their attraction and wanted to get him out of her plant as quickly as possible.

He swallowed, then turned his attention to his computer, to check his e-mail to see if he had gotten a response from his assistant. He didn't know why her rejection bothered him. Right now all they had was chemistry and his sketchy feeling that she belonged in his life. They really weren't suited for each other. He couldn't think of one thing they had in common. And she had a right to protect herself against getting hurt. She undoubtedly knew all about hurt from her divorce. He shouldn't expect her to stand still while he tried to figure out what to do. He wasn't sure he could give her a permanent relationship. He wasn't even sure he wanted a permanent relationship. Hell, he wasn't sure he had time for a permanent relationship. He couldn't be angry at her for protecting herself.

"Okay," he said, focusing his attention on the screen. "Elaine came through." He sneaked a peek at

Laurel. "This will speed things along, and it was a logical next step."

"What is it?"

"I e-mailed my assistant for everybody's password, so we can actually go into each individual's computer if we need to. But before we go that far, I also got a list of people who have access to the different sections of the software. Now we can see who has the ability to change amounts of purchase orders, and we can check them out first."

She leaned a little closer. "The information you got from your assistant was passwords and access lists?" she asked incredulously.

He glanced at her. "What did you think I wanted?"

Embarrassed, she backed away. "I don't know."

"You thought I was going for more personal information, didn't you."

She shrugged.

"Laurel, I'm sorry. I should have told you," he said, but those darn warning bells started ringing in his head again. If she was worried about his investigation, she had something to hide. If she had something to hide, not only should he be glad they hadn't gotten involved, but it might explain why she didn't want to have anything to do with him. Though curiosity nipped at his heels, Deke reminded himself he should respect her privacy, particularly since she'd all but rejected him, which made her life none of his business. He stomped down the questions that instantly formed and let the subject drop.

Unfortunately he couldn't seem to let it go. He didn't say anything out loud, but all day questions about her past nagged at him. By quitting time, after having spent the day watching her, admiring her cheerfulness and her ability to handle people, as much as her beauty, he concluded that nothing she had done could be bad enough for her to be fearful of an investigation. As easily as he had cleared her of theft based upon her innate goodness, Deke also cleared her of any ambiguous wrongdoing that might appear in her past, because it was just that—the past. She was now a stable, honest person, and anything she might have done ten years ago didn't matter.

And it wouldn't stop him from falling in love with her.

When he realized that, he finally understood that she believed that something in her past would prevent him from loving her, and that was why she had withdrawn. He also saw that both he and Laurel had decided against a relationship that could potentially be the best thing that ever happened to both of them.

But, if they were not going to pursue this attraction, he wanted them to do it with their eyes open and based on the facts. No guessing about what may or may not be in someone's past. No guessing about what may or may not happen in the future. They had to talk about this. Openly. Honestly. They had to have a conversation in which both of them were painfully truthful.

Then if she decided against the attraction, he would respect her feelings.

Laurel had successfully managed to avoid both him and the discussion every time they were alone for the next few days. But when he found her shooting pool in the basement rec room Thursday night, he wouldn't let her get away.

"We need to talk," Deke said from the stairs.

She shrugged, then hit the cue ball. "I don't see why."

"Because I think we're potentially throwing away something good."

"Trust me. Consider yourself to have dodged a bullet."

"See, that's just it," Deke said, sitting on the stair where he had stopped. "I don't think so. Every time I try to reconcile myself to avoiding you and ignoring this attraction, the feeling I get isn't dodging a bullet, but more like throwing away my future."

She stopped playing pool and stared at him. "You're kidding, right?"

He smiled, shook his head.

"Okay," she said, drawing in a deep breath. "Then let me explain some facts that might help you see why I think you should be running away from me. First, we come from two totally different worlds."

"That doesn't mean—"

She held up a hand to stop him. "That in and of itself might be something we could overcome—and I said *might*," she added emphatically. "But my past is messy enough that if you knew it, I don't think we would get to the stage where we would have to worry about our different worlds and lifestyles."

He shrugged. "I'm fifty percent of this equation. I don't think it's fair for you to make that choice for me. You have to tell me your past, Laurel. That's the fair thing to do."

"I know that," she said, and smacked the cue ball, which exploded into the three, which shot into the pocket as if it had been launched from a warship. Deke didn't think that boded well for her upcoming explanation.

But he didn't say anything. He simply waited.

After two more shots and at least four minutes, she said, "My mother wasn't exactly mother of the year."

Deke laughed. "Neither was mine."

"Yeah, well, mine had a drinking problem. *Had*," she emphasized. Deke was sure that was because to look at Judy now, to deal with her and spend time with her, you would never know it. Since the past was the past, Laurel was being careful not to prejudice his good opinion of her mother. "Because she couldn't always take care of me and my brother, we frequently found ourselves in foster homes."

"I'm sorry," Deke said, not knowing what else to say.

Studying the lay of the balls on the table, Laurel said, "It's certainly not your fault."

"No, and it's also part of the past."

"A very ugly past that a guy like you doesn't need in the résumé of his girlfriend."

He smiled at her use of the term, then said, "Maybe it would show people that I'm a thinker, that I don't dismiss someone because of an unfortunate past. Or maybe it would show people that I believe in the triumph of the human spirit."

She stared at him. "Anybody ever tell you you're an optimist?"

"Absolutely. But in this case it's warranted. After all, Laurel, look where you are."

She sighed. "I suppose."

"What else?"

"Well, the shortened version is that I got pregnant when I was sixteen, married Audra's father to cover the scandal and only got my high-school diploma through GED."

"You still got it."

"Yes, I still got it."

"And what happened with your husband?" At this she grew quiet again, and Deke knew this was the real crux of the issue. "Come on, Laurel, you're going to have to tell me sometime."

"Tell you what? That my ex was handsome like you?" She peered at him again. "Though not quite as handsome."

"See? There's one point in my favor."

She laughed.

"What else?"

"He was seven years older than me." She glanced at him.

Deke nodded.

"And he was very smart. He was the town smart guy who wanted to be more popular, so he got involved with the town's girl of questionable reputation—because everybody assumes kids in foster care are bad—and he ended up with more than he bargained for."

"And once you were married, you realized you had nothing in common and everything fell apart?" Deke speculated quietly.

"No, we actually stayed married a long time. And while we were married, he went from working as director of manufacturing at our plant to being offered a job as president of a plant in Texas."

Deke whistled. "Impressive."

She nodded. "I know. He scanned the Internet every day looking for his big break because he knew how intelligent he was and he knew that his break could be just around the corner."

"And when he got it, you didn't want to move to Texas."

She shook her head, hit the cue ball and knocked in

the six. "He didn't want to take us with him." She swallowed hard, but pretended great interest in the multicolored balls on the table, and Deke's heart melted. The stupid idiot jerk had dumped her. He'd left her and two adorable daughters behind.

"I told him I was pregnant with Sophie. He groaned and told me that sealed it. He didn't want a hick wife and two sniveling brats following him into Texas high society." She peeked at Deke again. "I didn't even know Texas had high society."

"There's a lot of oil in Texas," Deke explained. "Plus old money, old families." He shrugged. "They have their culture."

"And I didn't fit."

She completed her game with a resounding smack of her cue that resulted in sinking the last remaining ball, the eight. Deke rose from the steps and began pulling balls from the pockets.

"Laurel, that guy was a jerk. You can fit anywhere you want to."

She laughed prettily, lightening the mood, lifting Deke's spirits. "I don't think so."

He suddenly understood what she was saying. "Because you don't want to?"

"Because I don't want to pretend to be somebody I'm not."

"Good thinking," he said, and tapped her nose. "Eight ball?" he asked, picking up a cue.

"It's my best game."

"Good," Deke said, offering her the chance to break.

She declined with a quick shake of her head. "I like a challenge."

He broke, chose stripes, then examined the lay of

the balls for his next shot. "So what did you do after he left?"

"Struggled, scrambled for money and realized I would have to get promoted fast so I could earn enough to afford the house we'd bought with my ex-husband's salary."

"He doesn't pay child support?"

"He doesn't even acknowledge that he has kids."

"A real gentleman, I see."

"If that's a gentleman, I'll stay in my world."

"That's not a gentleman," Deke said, getting angry now. "Do you realize how quickly you judged me based on the behavior of your ex?"

Laurel laughed again. "I didn't judge *you.* I judged every executive trainee who came through my door. It's why I was a safe bet for caretaker." She laughed again. "Tom didn't have to worry that I'd be putting the moves on anyone."

"Right," Deke said, filled with annoyance at the thought that she might even consider kissing another executive trainee. "So now would you like to judge me on the truth?"

"Yeah, sure. Why not?"

"My father died when I was thirteen," Deke said, took his shot and missed everything on the table. He wasn't surprised. The feelings flowing through him now were odd, compelling and resonated with things he didn't even know existed. Driven by lust and on fire with unwarranted jealousy, it was difficult to think back to being a bewildered thirteen-year-old.

"I'm sorry."

"It was hard. Very hard. But more than that it was confusing. My mother fell apart, which is normal," he said, catching Laurel's gaze. "But then suddenly she was okay again. Solid as a brick wall, and she told me that was what I needed to be, too."

"Kind of like a Kennedy."

He considered that, then nodded. "We weren't running a country, but we were running a conglomerate. Thousands of people depended on us for their incomes. We didn't have the luxury of a long recuperation period."

"At thirteen you were considered to be one of the people running the company?"

"At thirteen I was the next person in line."

She stared at him incredulously. "What about your mother?"

He shook his head. "She's old school. Part of a patriarchal society. She did what my grandfather said."

"And he said you would run the show?"

"No, he said we would hire somebody to teach me how to run the show."

"What happened?"

"Six months after my father died, we hired Roger Smith, and six months after that, my mother was dating him."

"Ooohh! This is getting good."

Deke laughed. "Roger is short and bald. My mother loved him because he rescued her." Deke paused, caught Laurel's gaze. "He rescued us. When he married into the family, he could become head of the conglomerate. I didn't have to anymore. In a sense, he saved me."

"I never realized rich people had so many problems."

"Everybody has problems. Rich people just get to show up at theirs in better cars, wearing expensive clothes."

"So, do you want to take over the company?"

He didn't hesitate. "It's my heritage."

"That doesn't answer my question."

"Maybe I can't answer your question. I don't know what wanting something feels like." He caught her gaze again. "Except wanting you."

"Ah, maybe I'm the one thing you can't have. Maybe that's why I appeal to you."

He looked at her, the thick lustrous hair, the face of an angel, the body of a temptress, and he laughed. "I don't think so." He caught her by the waist and hauled her against him. "And neither do you. We have that chemistry that everybody talks about. No matter how much you try to dismiss me or ignore me, it doesn't go away."

"No," she said breathlessly. "It doesn't."

"And no matter how committed I am to my destiny, wanting you isn't going to go away, either."

She shook her head. "I don't think so."

"So what are we going to do about it?"

"Run?"

He laughed. "I've never run from anything in my life." He tipped her chin up until she was looking at him. "I'm certainly not running from the one thing I actually want."

He kissed her then. Long and hard and like a man who really was going after the first thing he had ever consciously wanted. And she kissed him back, answered everything he asked of her, not because he was the first man she'd ever wanted, but because she knew this was right. In her heart she knew it was right.

The only problem was, they had so many obstacles in their way and so many strikes against them she knew beyond a shadow of a doubt that if it worked, it would only be because they fought every step of the way. Because both of them had already spent a lifetime fighting, she wasn't sure either of them had the energy left to fight for love.

But more than that, with the commitments Deke Bertrim had, she wasn't sure he would have the time.

He might start this. He might want this. But he would never be able to finish.

Chapter Eight

Deke realized that whether they had intended to do it or not, he and Laurel had made a commitment and, in a sense, begun planning a future together.

He ran his thumb across Laurel's upper lip, which he had dampened with his kiss, and stood amazed that all this was happening. He had dated lots of women. In Pittsburgh he was actually something of a ladies' man, but this was different. All his other relationships, even the ones that were physical, were predictable relationships that fit into his life. What he had with Laurel was not predictable or expected. It was something that he wanted. *Wanted.* For the first time in his life he was pursuing something that had nothing to do with rhyme or reason, only desire, yearnings and need. Nothing safe. Nothing predictable. Even as it exhilarated him, it scared the hell out of him.

"I'm going home for the weekend," he said slowly, carefully.

She nodded, but Deke could tell she missed his meaning.

"Laurel, I want you and the girls to come with me."

Laurel froze in his arms. "What?"

"I want you to come with me."

"I—"

"You have to."

In a way, Laurel understood that she did. It was something like jumping into a cold swimming pool. The quicker she got it over with the better, because the reward would be well worth the jolt of reality. And if it wasn't, she would immediately know to get out of the water. Though Laurel genuinely believed Deke wouldn't be able to fulfill this commitment, she owed it to him to be sure. Looking into his striking blue eyes, she also knew she owed it to herself.

At breakfast Friday morning they explained to the girls that they were going to visit Deke's house. Sophie decided they were going to his house because he had spent so much time at theirs, and Laurel let that explanation alone. But Audra was much more attentive. Though she didn't voice them, Laurel saw the questions in her little girl's eyes.

After the regularly scheduled Saturday-morning softball game, they went home and changed to begin the drive to Pittsburgh. But when they met in the kitchen, Laurel and the girls were dressed in shorts and summer-weight shirts, but Deke was wearing dress shorts and a casual, but expensive shirt, and Laurel had her first jolt of reality.

"You look fine," Deke said, apparently responding to the expression on her face.

"You're sure?"

"Absolutely," he said, then almost kissed her, but

he held back, and Laurel suddenly saw that this relationship of theirs was so new that even her children didn't know about it.

Laurel relaxed, recognizing that her various and sundry concerns might be nothing more than part of the newness of the situation. But when they pulled into a lane, then went through an iron gate and traveled another mile before they came to a mansion, Laurel knew that newness had nothing to do with her apprehension.

Mingled with her own fear, though, she felt a shot of unexpected empathy. Her very sensitive, very sweet new love interest grew up in this cold impersonal house. She suddenly understood why he was drawn to her, and also recognized that she couldn't let him down. He was looking for emotion, passion, acceptance, happiness, anger, *everything*. And she had those in abundance. She was looking for stability, sensitivity, kindness and strength. He had those in abundance. In their own way, they matched. This was not an accident.

And she couldn't turn back or turn away any more than he could.

"Would you please let Mother know we're here?" Deke asked of the uniformed woman who immediately appeared at the door. She nodded once and left, and before Laurel could even reach down to grab her suitcase a man in a black suit appeared and took the handle from her.

"Sam, could you see that my things get to my room, and please put Ms. Hillman's things and her daughters' in the guest apartment?"

"Yes, sir," the man said, nodded once to acknowledge Laurel and left the room.

Laurel couldn't help it. She shivered.

"Cold?"

"Intimidated."

"Don't let Samuel or Mrs. Orlavski fool you. Deep down they're both very nice people."

"I'm sure," Laurel said, then she smiled at Deke. He smiled back and took her hand, ready to lead her down a long corridor to the left. Instead, he stopped, stooped in front of Audra and Sophie and said, "I'm taking you back to meet my mother."

"You really are going to marry our mom, aren't you?"

This time it was Audra who asked the question, not Sophie, but Laurel wanted to shrivel up and die, anyway.

"Could be," Deke said, glancing up at Laurel with a smile. "But what you need to know is that before two people make a commitment like that, they try to get to know each other. That's what we're doing here. Everybody is trying to get to know everybody else."

"Oh," Audra said, appreciating the explanation.

Sophie only grinned and hugged her bear.

At the moment Laurel wished she had a bear to hug, too.

Deke guided them down a long dim corridor to a room that Laurel considered too big to be a den and too fancy to be a study. A man in his sixties sat behind a huge cherry desk, and a somewhat younger woman sat on a leather sofa. Their gazes had swung to the opening door, but once Deke appeared, both bounced from their seats. "Deke!"

"Hello, Mother," Deke said, and kissed the cheek of the petite, elegantly dressed woman.

"Roger."

"Deke," Roger Smith said, shaking his stepson's hand. "This must be Laurel."

"And daughters," Laurel said, accepting a quick cool hug from Deke's mother and a handshake from his stepfather.

"The older girl is Audra. And the little one is Sophie."

"This is Fred," Sophie said, introducing her bear when all eyes turned to her. Laurel's lips twisted to hide a smile. Just as Laurel had taken attention from herself by introducing her children, Sophie had taken the attention from herself by introducing her bear.

"Well, aren't you two just the cutest things!" Deke's mother said with a gasp. "Children," she said, laughing shakily. "Deke, you never told us Laurel had children."

"I asked Mrs. O. to prepare the apartment."

"She never mentioned that," Mrs. Smith said before turning to Laurel. "My name is Miriam, by the way. Everyone calls me Mimi."

"Thank you," Laurel said, not knowing what else to say or how else to act. At the moment she could happily have jumped out of her skin.

"Would you like to see my garden?"

"Yes," Laurel said, glad for the diversion. But as they walked toward the French doors that opened onto a huge patio, she heard Deke explaining the situation at the plant to his stepfather.

"So, right now, I have a partial list of passwords and access codes. Elaine is having a little trouble getting the rest of the list from Personnel. That bothers me."

"Are you thinking someone in Corporate might be involved?"

Deke shook his head. "I don't know what to think."

"I do," Laurel said suddenly, turning from the

French doors toward the conversation behind her. "Jim Franklin's been dragging his feet about turning in his department's passwords. That might be why you're having trouble. He could be withholding his information deliberately."

"You didn't tell me that," Deke said.

Laurel shrugged. "I never put it all together. Mostly because I only hear Jim getting reminded about turning in his lists at our supervisors' meetings. Those are held once a month. But we have one coming up this week, and I'm pretty sure he'll have to be reminded again."

"So this Franklin fellow is starting to look good for at least being in on the deal?" Roger asked.

"That's what it seems like," Deke said.

"Damn it, I hate things like this," Roger said, then took a seat behind the desk again. "Undoubtedly we're going to be firing someone." He paused, looked at Deke and said, "You know this might get really ugly."

"I know," Deke said, nodding, and Laurel almost went over and took the seat beside him, but Mimi tapped her arm.

"The gardens, dear?"

"Oh, yes. Yes. I'm sorry."

Laurel turned to face Mimi with a smile, but met an odd look that was part curiosity and part condemnation. For Deke's sake she listened with rapt attention to Mimi's descriptions of flowers and shrubs and who planted what when, but she never lost the feeling that Deke's mother totally disapproved of her. And her kids. When Sophie broke the antique vase in the front foyer, Laurel was certain of it.

But when she walked past the study on her way to find Deke to try to apologize and figure out how she could make things right and overheard Deke and his parents talking, Laurel decided she and Deke had made a huge mistake. Not only was his mother infuriated that Deke seemed to have made up his mind about Laurel too quickly and without sufficient consideration, but she thought Laurel's business knowledge bordered on vulgar.

"Her husband left her, Mother," she heard Deke explain with barely controlled anger. "I think it's admirable that she not only got a job to support herself and her children, but she got her GED by going to school at night so she could be promoted into a supervisory capacity."

"She has a general education diploma? She didn't even go to high school!" Mimi said with a gasp.

"Now, Mimi," Roger interrupted, but Laurel left. She didn't need to hear more because Deke's parents were right. She didn't fit. Her kids didn't fit. And Deke was getting the third degree. This was a mistake. A big, big mistake. And the sooner they admitted that the better.

When they drove home late Sunday night, Laurel could feel waves of tension radiating off Deke. But because it was inappropriate to discuss the situation in front of the children, she waited until after the girls were in bed before she went in search of him. Oddly enough she found him stretched out on the sofa in her family room. His hands were arranged behind his neck, and his eyes were wide open as he stared blankly at the ceiling.

"That's not how a nap is supposed to look."

"I'm not napping," Deke said, and quickly sat up. Laurel could swear she saw him struggling to put a smile on his face, and she knew what she had to do.

"We failed," she said simply.

"No. No," Deke disagreed, obviously understanding her vague comment. "That was just the preliminary round. Mother is standoffish with everybody. Remember, she's old school. She wouldn't even attempt to run the company after my father died. She's going to come around," Deke insisted.

But Laurel shook her head. "She shouldn't have to come around. For Pete's sake, Deke, you live in a palace. My kids would make mincemeat out of your furniture in three days. Forget about antique vases. And frankly, I don't think Samuel likes kids. Sophie tried to talk to him and he almost ran in the opposite direction."

"The staff is directed not to speak with visitors unless they have specific questions."

"There, see? We didn't know that. We don't belong there, Deke." Laurel combed her fingers through her hair because this hurt much more than she was letting on. It was insulting and demeaning to realize your behavior wasn't good enough. It was insulting to realize that getting a job could be considered pedestrian behavior. Actually it was infuriating. Deke's mother was a snob. And Laurel couldn't promise that she wouldn't someday tell her that. So, Laurel wouldn't put him in the middle of two battling women any more than she would ask him to choose. Rather than put him in that awful no-win situation, she would simply put an end to this madness before it went any further. It was better for her to endure the hurt of losing.

And she would hurt. She felt she was throwing away the best thing that had ever happened to her.

"You're refusing to try?" Deke asked incredulously.

"I did try," Laurel said, incredulous herself. "Deke, you saw what happened. Sophie broke a vase. Audra didn't eat she was so scared. You mother thinks I'm vulgar." She paused because her voice was rising with every word and none of this was Deke's fault. Unfortunately that meant he couldn't change any of it, which meant they had hit the end of the line. "It's wrong, Deke. We both knew it wouldn't work. I'm sorry."

"Laurel, we've known each other only a little over three weeks," Deke began.

But Laurel grabbed his argument and twisted it even before he had a chance to say it. "Even better. Neither one of us has put too much into this, so neither one of us loses too much."

She turned and walked out of the room, not giving him a chance to argue with her. When he didn't come after her, Laurel knew she was right. He might not have wanted it to be this way, but their mismatch, no matter how tempting, was still a mismatch.

The next morning when Deke came to the table looking like a man who hadn't slept, Laurel ignored the longing she had to comfort him. When he didn't say two words at work, she didn't push him. When he didn't take lunch, she expected he was going to access his intercompany e-mail and check to see if his assistant had had any more luck with getting his information. But the next night, when he still hadn't spoken two words or shaved in two days, she confronted him on the back-porch swing.

"You can't be that upset," she said, taking a seat beside him. "We didn't know each other long enough for you to feel this badly."

"But I do."

She believed him, because she felt as awful as he did. She was confused, numb, lonely. It just didn't seem fair.

"I don't know what to say, Deke. This isn't either of our fault. We have the same problem that's plagued lovers since the beginning of time. We come from two different worlds, and I don't fit into yours. There's no help for it. No way to fix it."

"I don't believe that," Deke disagreed, sounding more determined than she'd ever heard him sound. "I think if we wanted to, we could work around our life-style differences. Hell, if we wanted to, we could change the way we live." He paused, caught her shoulders and looked into her eyes, his expression so hopeful her breath caught in her chest. "Don't you see? We're two adults at the beginning of a new relationship. We can make it anything we want."

Away from his mother, the mansion and the broken vase, and every bit as eager to assuage his hurt as she was to get comfort herself, Laurel believed him. She wanted to believe him. "I see what you're saying."

"You do?"

At his incredulous tone, Laurel smiled. "It was *your* determination that convinced me."

"Good, because I am determined," Deke said. "I wasn't going to push you, but tonight at dinner I decided I wasn't taking no for an answer."

He pulled her into his arms and kissed her, and for the first time in two days Laurel felt whole again. She didn't know what it was about this man, but she needed him. Even as he inspired her to new heights of passion, raining kisses down her throat, Laurel felt the strength and security of him. Need burned inside her, pure feminine greedy lust, but rather than be afraid, she felt strong, confident. Because she could trust him. When they made love, it would be as passionate as a thunderstorm, because inside they had the security of love.

But that thought stopped her. The only real security they had was the knowledge that they felt the same way. Right now, right at this minute, they wanted the same things. But that wasn't a guarantee of anything permanent. One of these days Deke would wake up and realize there were just too many differences in their lifestyles, too many issues that confronted them, and he would regret getting involved with her.

Still, it was too late to guard her heart. She already loved him, and she was going to get hurt.

Chapter Nine

"So then what happened?"

Laurel stirred cream into the cup of coffee her sister-in-law, Wanda, had given her. Jeff, Wanda's husband and Laurel's brother, was bowling. Audra and Deke had softball practice and Judy had taken Sophie shopping. Laurel had decided to take advantage of the opportunity to talk with someone who might not understand, but who could at least sympathize with her predicament.

"For some reason or other Sophie picked up speed, rounded the corner with a little more energy than necessary and her shoulder caught a corner of a small table."

Wanda groaned and shook her head. Her bouncy blond ponytail swung back and forth. Her blue eyes darkened with concern. "This doesn't have a good ending, does it?"

"No. A vase went crashing to the floor."

"And his mother was angry?"

Laurel shrugged. "Oh, no. It was only a priceless vase. And Sophie's such a sweet girl, how could she be angry?"

"You're being facetious, right?"

"Completely."

"This isn't sounding good at all."

"The woman thinks I'm vulgar because I work. Audra didn't eat she was so intimidated by the house and the servants. Deke and I didn't spend two minutes together. I almost got the feeling it was inappropriate for men and women to mix and mingle."

Wanda giggled. "Maybe it is. What the heck do we know about how rich people live? We're lucky to be able to stick money into our retirement savings through payroll deduction. Forget about stock. Forget about owning a company. Forget about having a maid and butler. Our kids don't know how to behave around priceless art, because we have none. And our men don't retire to the study to smoke cigars and sip brandy, because we can't afford them. You're not nuts and you're not wrong. You simply don't have the experience to blend into his world."

Laurel sagged with defeat. "Thank you very much for your vote of confidence."

"Hey, truth is truth. I didn't say you wouldn't ever get the experience."

"I'm not sure I *want* the experience," Laurel interrupted, agitated now. "We spent over forty-eight hours in the same house, yet we didn't talk to each other. What kind of life is that?"

Wanda was thoughtful for a few seconds, then she grinned. "You see what you're saying, don't you?"

Laurel shook her head.

"His life isn't so hot and you don't want it."

"I already figured that out. I didn't need you to tell me we're going to fail."

"You're not going to fail. What you're going to do is make a different lifestyle choice."

"I don't get it."

"Well, Deke is perfectly comfortable with you. You've even told me that he's admitted he's happier now than he's ever been."

Laurel nodded.

"So in a kind of backhanded way, the two of you are rejecting his parents' lifestyle or maybe choosing yours."

"Omigosh!" Laurel suddenly understood what Wanda was saying. "You're right."

"The only question is, does Deke recognize this?"

Laurel paused in her elation to consider that. "I don't know, but he did say we could pick any kind of life we wanted."

"That's a good sign," Wanda said, then added, "Did he want you to go to his family home to meet his parents, or did he want you to go to begin the process of fitting in?"

Laurel slumped to a seat. "I don't know."

"Well, it really doesn't matter," Wanda said with a shrug. "The point is, you have to make sure Deke sees and understands that there's a difference. He's happy with you, in your world. *Nobody* is happy in his world. Heck, it doesn't even sound as if his parents are happy. If it comes down to a choice, you have to set things up so he picks your life over his."

"You're right," Laurel said, bent and gave her sister-in-law a big smacking kiss on the cheek. "You're always right," she added, grabbing her sweater from the back of her chair before she darted toward the kitchen door. But when she reached it, old fears about her ex-husband resurfaced and she stopped dead in her tracks. "Exactly how do I set things up so that he chooses me?"

"He's already chosen *you*," Wanda said with a laugh. "What you need to do is make him see how comfortable he is in your world, how much he likes your world and how happy he is. So, that if it comes down to a choice between the two places to live—and it is going to come down to a choice—he will pick your house, your world, and only go back to his for visits." Wanda paused and gave Laurel a concerned look. "You can survive *visits* to his world, can't you?"

"Sure. *I* can. But I'm not sure the kids can."

"Don't worry about that right now. That's a bridge you can cross later. For now, your mission—should you decide to accept it—is to show that man he is exactly where he belongs for the rest of his life."

Deke became a little suspicious after the fourth homemade pie. When Laurel roused the parents to give him a round of applause after a Saturday-morning game because he was such a good coach, he was sure something was up. When she came right out and told him that he fit into her world, Deke suddenly saw what it was. He knew the weekend with his parents had upset her. In a lot of ways it upset him, too. His parents were having trouble accepting her, and she didn't like them. Because he could appreciate that his parents might need time to get accustomed to the situation, Deke hadn't thought too much about it.

Apparently Laurel had.

He knew he had told her they could choose the way they wanted to live, but he didn't mean they had to choose one lifestyle or the other. He thought they would come to some kind of compromise, not hold an election.

"I got a new list from Elaine," Deke announced when the rest of the shipping-and-receiving crew had deserted the cage for their break. "Do you think you can get some overtime authorized?"

Laurel turned to him with a bright smile. "Yes. Sure. Absolutely. If there's one thing about a small town I can guarantee, it's that people easily make accommodations for each other."

Deke frowned. "I know that, Laurel."

"See? Even you know it, and you've only been around for a few weeks."

"Are you going to talk to me about what's bothering you?" he asked, watching her flit around their work area as if she couldn't decide what to do next, or maybe as if she had no real excuse to stay in the work area and was trying to think of one.

"There's nothing bothering me," she said, and again her voice was unnaturally cheery. "I'm fine. Really fine."

"Uh-huh," he said, but he knew that wasn't true. Not only did he have the instinct that the trip to his home upset her and she was campaigning to stay in Maryland, but now her constant chatter about small-town life was making him suspect she was concerned about what people would think when word of their relationship got out. Because their romance wasn't common knowledge at the plant, or even among the townsfolk, Deke could only conclude his parents' reaction made her realize people would talk about them, and she was fretting about that. Of course, if they did decide to marry and moved to Pittsburgh, all this would be irrelevant.

But he didn't think this was the time or place to bring up that consolation, so he went back to work and allowed *her* to go back to work.

He asked her again after dinner if something was bothering her, and again her smile was too bright, her voice too cheery. Since Judy and the girls were just in the other room watching television, Deke didn't force the issue. Instead, he began to do a little too much thinking himself. If Laurel concluded she couldn't handle the embarrassment of everyone knowing she had basically lived with him while they debated a relationship, she could change her mind about him again. After all, they were still at the point in their relationship where no one would get too hurt if they chose not to pursue their attraction—no one, that is, but him. He wouldn't be mortally wounded, but even thinking about spending the rest of his life without her gave Deke an awful empty feeling. He didn't know how he knew, but he knew this was right and good, and somehow he had to convince Laurel of that.

By the time Judy had gone home and the girls were in bed, he was as nervous as a boy on his first date. Worse, he had now decided against confronting her directly. He didn't want to give her the opportunity to break off with him again, because he knew that was the quick and easy way out for both of them. No matter what problems they faced, he was sure they could overcome them. But he knew she wasn't so sure. And the only way to give her sufficient faith in him that she would have the courage to stick with this relationship was through example.

He waited until she was sitting in front of the television, comfortable, relaxed and done with her child-care duties before he said, "You know, you're not the first person I've ever been serious about."

That got her attention. She fixed her huge green eyes on him as if he had just grown a second head.

"Why are you so surprised?" he asked with a laugh. "I'm not exactly repulsive, you know."

"I know. It's just that your life seems so... sheltered."

"Closed," Deke corrected, then took the seat beside her on the sofa and put his arm around her shoulders so he could pull her against him. "At least that's what it seems to you. But I was actually voted Pittsburgh's most eligible bachelor three years in a row. I met women when I was on the road with the team. My family belonged to two country clubs, and at Harvard I dated plenty of women."

Laurel peered at him in dismay. "You know, when we first started this conversation, I got the impression you were trying to cheer me up."

He conceded that with a nod.

"It's not working," she said. "Change tactics. Telling me about being voted most eligible bachelor, going to Harvard and belonging to country clubs only reminds me how wrong we are for each other."

"It shouldn't."

She stared at him. "You are really out of touch with reality."

"Not at all. And that's what I'm trying to tell you. I think—" he stopped her when she groaned and tried to move away "—that you assume that because my life has been so sheltered or maybe directed that I haven't had enough experiences to make the kind of commitment both of us seem to want to make."

She relaxed against his arm. "Could be. At least that's part."

"Then let me put your mind to rest. I know what we're getting into. I had a relationship with a woman I intended to marry when I was twenty-one. Brittany had been first in her class. She was a champion horsewoman. She modeled and she was in law school."

Laurel gaped at him. "This is supposed to make me feel better? You're back to making me feel all wrong for you again. Stop while you're ahead."

"You're going to find all this out, anyway. Besides, the story doesn't have a happy ending…well, at least I didn't think so at the time. Now I realize everything happened for a reason. A good reason. Can I finish?"

She nodded reluctantly.

Deke continued. "Because my parents talked me into delaying the wedding at least until Brittany was out of law school—"

"Your parents talked you out of getting married?" Laurel asked in dismay.

"They couldn't have talked me out of it if I hadn't agreed. I still hadn't graduated. Brittany had years of school ahead of her. Getting engaged was fine. Getting married was jumping the gun."

"So you broke off with her?"

"Nope. I only asked her to postpone the wedding. She broke off with me."

"Oh," Laurel said, sounding confused.

"Which proves I've not only been in love, but I've had my heart broken."

"Which proves you're not afraid to risk your heart again?"

"Well, not really," Deke said quietly. "I don't want to get my heart broken again, so I'm more careful. I'm not jumping into this relationship with you lightly. And that's the biggest part of my point."

She nodded.

"But there's a little bit more to the story. For one, Brittany didn't just break up with me. She started dating my friends. Not only that, but she ended up marrying one of them."

"Ouch."

"There's more. She dumped my friend after about a year and took him to the cleaners."

"You were engaged to this woman?"

Deke nodded. "She was totally and completely wrong for me."

"And your parents wisely pointed that out."

"No. I saw it myself because of her behavior after we broke up. And I didn't go back with her when I had the chance, even though I missed our relationship desperately. Proof again that I'm not naive, or sheltered, or even confused. I know what I'm doing. My parents never said one word to me about Brittany, except to agree with me about postponing the wedding."

"So you're not just telling me that you know what you're doing, you're telling me your parents are going to let you make your own choice."

Exasperated, he sighed. "You're missing the point. I'm thirty-three. I don't *need* my parent's approval. I've been in a relationship that didn't work. I now know most of the signs. I've dated lots of women and never wanted to make a permanent commitment—until now. Until you."

The very sweet way he said what he said made Laurel swallow. If Pittsburgh's most eligible bachelor three years in a row had well-practiced lines, he wasn't using them on her. As always, he was being honest.

"I'm sorry that you thought I doubted you, but I didn't really doubt you."

"Sure you did," he said, then kissed her nose.

"No," Laurel said, convicted by his honesty because she hadn't exactly been honest with him. "I doubt myself."

"Oh," he said, stiffening and shifting away from her. "I'm sorry. I didn't realize you weren't sure of your feelings for me."

"I *am* sure of my feelings for you. Every day they seem to grow by leaps and bounds. Most days they scare the heck out of me they're so strong."

"But…"

"But I don't fit into your world."

"We'll work around that."

"How?"

"I don't know. But I know that something this right will have a solution." He took her chin in his fingers and lifted her face until she was looking directly at him. "I know neither one of us is at the point where we can say we're in love. I know we have a long way to go before we really understand everything we're feeling, but, Laurel, please don't borrow trouble."

He cupped her face with his hands and pressed his mouth to hers. And when their lips met, Laurel was instantly filled with an intense longing, but more than that, she was now beginning to feel the sense of rightness and destiny that Deke had felt all along. She had never been drawn to anyone the way she was drawn to Deke. She had never felt closer to anyone. And she had never wanted anyone the way she wanted him.

Her bad-girl days had existed only in the minds of the local gossips, and for all her ex-husband's supposed lack of sophistication, he had actually seduced her. But

with Deke, Laurel didn't believe she needed to be co-
erced or coaxed. Kissing him coaxed her. Touching
him filled her with need. When his hands slid from her
cheeks, down her neck, to her shoulders so he could
draw her closer, it was everything she could do not to
shiver.

He deepened the kiss and she shifted on the sofa and
began to slide backward. The hint of an invitation was
all Deke seemed to need, and the temperature of the
kiss hitched a notch as his hands began a slow cautious
journey from her shoulders to her arms and then back
up again. There was no doubt in her mind that he
would only go as far as she wanted to go. Her one
question was, how far did she want him to go? For
what, exactly, was she ready? For what were *they*
ready?

The ringing of the phone brought them back to reality. Dazed, Laurel just stared at Deke for several seconds and he stared back at her. Any time she wondered
if they were going to make it, all she had to do was
look into his eyes and the question no longer mattered.

The phone rang again.

Deke cleared his throat and pushed off the couch to
get the phone in the kitchen. Bewitched and bedazzled,
Laurel stayed on the sofa.

"Hello?" he said, then paused to listen. "Oh, God.
No. No, I'll be right there. Sam, I know that Roger has
a list of instructions in the safe behind the desk in the
den. Get them out and get them to the hospital. I'll be
there as soon as I can."

When Laurel heard the word *hospital,* she jumped
off the sofa. "What's wrong?" she asked the second
Deke disconnected the call.

"Roger's had a heart attack."

"Oh, no!"

"I don't know how bad it is, but I do know my mother can't handle this alone." He combed his fingers through his hair. "Hell, she falls apart so easily Roger even wrote a list of instructions of what to do in case he ever couldn't speak for himself. I told Sam where they were. He's taking them to the hospital so the doctors at least have some idea of Roger's wishes."

"Is his condition that bad?" Laurel whispered.

Deke shook his head. "I don't know, but I've got to get to Pittsburgh."

"Of course. Go," Laurel said, rubbing his arm in support. "Is there anything I can do?"

Deke sighed. "No. I'm sure everything's going to be fine. I just need to get home and supervise."

"Okay," Laurel said, but when Deke left the kitchen to go to his room to grab a few things before he started home, she sank onto a kitchen chair.

She was banking on his being able to shift from his life into hers, and though he could do that to a point, there was only so far anyone could shift out of his life. He had a mother who needed someone to care for her and a stepfather who was sick.

Not to mention a conglomerate that somebody had to run.

Deke came jogging down the back steps with his duffel bag and Laurel rose for a quick kiss. "I'll be back as soon as I can."

"Don't be silly," Laurel admonished gently. "You stay as long as you're needed."

"Right," he said, gave her another quick kiss and rushed out the door.

Laurel stood staring at the closed door, wondering who was kidding whom. If he had too many commitments to stay in her world and she didn't fit into his, did it really matter how much they loved each other?

Actually he never did say he loved her.

In fact, he made a point of reminding her that neither one of them could say it yet.

Chapter Ten

"So when is Deke coming back?"

Laurel looked across the breakfast table at her mother. Deke had already been gone almost two weeks, and though he had called several times a day for the first few days, his calls had dwindled to once a day, and now two days had gone by without a word. "I don't know."

"How is his stepfather?"

"Recovering."

"How's his mother handling everything?"

That was the sticking point. His mother had completely fallen apart. Deke didn't have the authority to make decisions for Graham Industries, and though Tom Baxter had a limited power of attorney, he didn't feel comfortable replacing Deke's stepfather. And Roger Smith needed at least four weeks of bed rest. Right now, Deke had explained, he, Roger and Tom were trying to figure out how to get everything done without involving Roger. But Laurel suspected that what they

were really debating was whether or not to officially
hand over the controls to Deke. On the good side, he
could be refusing the promotion. On the bad side, either
Tom Baxter or Roger Smith might not think he was
ready. Since Deke hadn't called in two days, she didn't
know which it was.

Deke had invited Laurel to come to Pittsburgh the
first weekend, but she couldn't leave the girls and
didn't think it was appropriate to add to the stress of
the household by bringing her two children. As far as
Laurel was concerned, Deke's stepfather's heart attack
was pointing out things that Laurel had suspected all
along, but couldn't make Deke see. There was no way
to mesh their two worlds.

To keep herself from thinking too much about the
situation, which appeared to deteriorate even further as
the days wore on, Laurel found the list of passwords
and the list of who had access to what software that
Deke's assistant had e-mailed to him. She began checking and cross-checking to see if she could figure out
what was going on with inventory and got exactly nowhere for the two days she spent reading and rereading
the lists. But on her way home from a late-night trip
to the store to get milk and bread, she saw Jim Franklin's truck parked at the back of the plant and she
changed the direction of her search.

Rather than try to ascertain who had the ability to
pull off a scheme to steal from the plant, she decided
that if she could figure out what had been done, eventually the guilty party would be obvious. As if she was
creating a geometric theory, she began to hypothesize
that someone from Purchasing, whom she labeled X,
and Jim Franklin, supervisor of Inventory, were in ca-
hoots.

With their abilities and accesses in mind, she monitored six purchase orders for goods received and discovered that nothing happened until after the bills were paid for the items purchased. Then, magically, once the invoices were closed, the amounts on the original purchase orders decreased to match the lower quantity that Laurel found in Inventory. When she tracked the process through the various computer procedures that would have to be performed to accomplish the switches, she discovered the changes had been made on the unit in inventory.

It wasn't solid proof, but it was enough information to suspect that someone from Inventory and someone from Purchasing had set up a little scheme to steal from the plant. A more thorough audit would undoubtedly uncover the specifics, but Laurel was convinced that she had at least pinned down what was being done and narrowed the list of suspects.

Because Deke was preoccupied with his family situation, Laurel didn't mention her discoveries or her theories to him when he called. In her excitement she actually convinced herself that she was only longing for him to come home because she was eager to tell him her news. So when he burst through the door almost three weeks after his stepfather's heart attack and Laurel turned from the stove to see him, she wasn't expecting her heart to stop or her nervous system to go into overdrive.

She also wasn't expecting that he would grab her around the shoulders and hoist her up for a long passionate kiss.

She wasn't expecting any of it, but deep down inside she had been yearning for it, aching for him to come home for reasons that had nothing to do with work and stolen inventory.

"I'm so glad to be back," he said, holding her tightly.

"I'm glad you're back, too," Laurel said, her eyes filling with tears.

"I take it you missed me?"

"I missed you."

"Good," he said.

The obvious relief in his voice revived Laurel's confidence and she leaned back so she could see his face. "I really missed you and I have some exciting news."

"So do I," Deke said, tossing his duffel bag onto the third step of the stairway off the kitchen. "I attended a fund-raiser my mother was chairing, and for the first time in the charity's history, they topped a million dollars in donations."

"Oh," Laurel said, surprised not only by the amount of the donations, but also that his excitement was over something she didn't consider important, given that his stepfather had had a heart attack and the family's billion-dollar conglomerate didn't have a leader. In fact, she was confused about how they had time to attend a fund-raiser with Roger in the hospital.

"It was a dinner dance with a hefty seating fee, but benefactors were more or less encouraged to write checks on the spot, and with my mother and me working the room, we did unbelievably well. She was ecstatic."

"I'm sure she was," Laurel said, trying not to sound as if she was baffled and bothered, because she already knew things worked differently in Deke's world than they did in hers. "Who stayed with your stepfather through this?"

"Well, Tom volunteered, but Roger didn't want to risk Mother's event failing, so he insisted we all go." Apparently having caught something in her voice, Deke added, "He had full-time nurses."

"Oh."

"Anyway, the fund-raiser was great. I had a fabulous time. I saw people I haven't seen in years," he said, then opened the refrigerator, rummaging for food. "Two of the girls I dated in high school just got out of ten-year marriages. I had very enlightening talks with both of them. And then at the golf tournament held the next day, I ended up playing with one of their ex-husbands."

"That sounds sticky."

"It could have been, but Connor mentioned right up front that he knew I knew his ex-wife and he hoped I wouldn't hold anything against him."

"How civil," Laurel said, her heart sinking as she sat down.

"It's not 'civil,' it's open-minded," Deke said as he tossed bread and cold cuts onto the table to make a sandwich. "We all rotate in the same circles. Everybody has to be open-minded."

"I'm sure."

Laurel supposed it was the tone of her voice that caught his attention, but she couldn't help it. What he was describing as open-minded seemed almost fake to her. Worse, she couldn't get beyond the fact that for a guy who was supposed to have missed her, Deke sounded as if he'd had the time of his life—dinner dances, golf outings. It appeared that what he really missed was being in Pittsburgh, and he had taken great advantage of every day he was there. Proof that though he might fit into her world, he liked his own world and obviously anticipated returning. Unfortunately, with this new round of information about the people in his life, Laurel was more certain than ever that she would never fit in.

"What's wrong?"

"I'm anxious to talk about the things I discovered at the plant, that's all," Laurel said, lying, and inwardly cringing because normally she wouldn't do that. Normally she would admit that the people in his life sounded like phonies and she thought it was heartless that his mother attended a fund-raiser while his stepfather lay in a hospital bed.

"I'm curious to know," Deke said, taking a seat after he had finished preparing his sandwich. "What did you find out?"

"That the purchase orders are being changed after the bills for the goods are paid. Which means that someone from Purchasing is ordering extra, someone from Inventory is pulling it from stock and monitoring the purchase order to discover when the bill is paid. Then once it's paid, someone from Inventory is changing the amount ordered."

"I followed you right up to where you're sure someone from Inventory is the one changing the purchase order. How do you know it's somebody from Inventory?"

"The system logs every person who goes into the software, but in this case it identified the *computer* used to go into the software because there are several people in Inventory who use that computer, so it's not listed under a single person's name. That means that though we don't know exactly who is changing the purchase orders, we do know it was the computer in Inventory being used to make the changes."

"But not who was doing it."

"Right. I have no clue who is doing it and just a bare-bones idea of what's being done."

Deke smiled. "You have enough information to supply to an audit team so that we can verify exactly what's been ordered and then taken."

"But we still don't know who is doing it," Laurel reminded him, beginning to panic. It suddenly dawned on her that with the investigation progressed to the point where an audit team could take over to find specifics, Deke could leave. In fact, he *should* leave. He was needed at home.

"Who's running the corporation?" Laurel asked, tracing one of the flowers in the print of her plastic kitchen tablecloth.

"Tom's got power of attorney, but every day my stepfather is a little more alert, so every day he's doing more and more of the things Tom brings into the hospital."

"Do you think that's good for him?"

"At this point it would be worse not to let him at least do part of his normal work. Otherwise, he would worry himself to death."

"I see," Laurel said, though she didn't. If it was *her* stepfather, she would insist he rest and not trouble himself with work. But Deke's stepfather would be worse off being banished from work. Her mother wouldn't have let her father alone in a hospital room while she attended a formal charity dinner. And if two of her friends' ex-husbands wanted to play golf with her, they'd have to watch out for flyaway golf clubs.

"You have that look on your face that something's bothering you again," Deke said quietly.

"No. Everything's fine," Laurel said, but watching her eyes as she spoke, Deke knew she was lying.

He also recognized that he had been away for three weeks, that she worried they weren't suited to each other, and that she would always be one step away from running away from him and giving up on their relationship unless he forced her to stay. He couldn't force her to marry him—they really weren't ready for that yet—and asking her might only spook her more.

But Deke did know a way to commit her to him. It was time to take their relationship to the next level. They both wanted it, and it would be the proof of the commitment that they needed.

It amazed Deke that after three weeks away, he still felt comfortable in Laurel's small hometown. He remembered directions as if he had been driving for more than the one short month he had lived here before his stepfather's heart attack. He felt incredibly at ease striding up the sidewalk to Laurel's brother's home and even face-to-face with her sister-in-law, Wanda—pink spongy curlers, red plaid robe and all.

"Hi, Wanda," he said, giving her his best smile when she answered her front door. "You probably don't remember me, but I'm—"

"I know who you are," she interrupted, then opened her screen door and invited him inside. "I'm just a little confused about why you're here."

"I need a favor."

Her eyebrows rose and she gave him a baffled look.

"I'm just going to cut right to the heart of the matter, here," he said, trying not to be intimidated by the fact that she didn't seem to like him. "I've been gone for three weeks, Laurel and I need some time alone, Judy isn't a good overnight baby-sitter, and I was hoping I could convince you to help by keeping the girls for Laurel and me tonight.''

A few seconds passed while Wanda obviously digested that information. Her gaze took a leisurely perusal of his face as she apparently assessed his character, since it was clear why he would want an entire night without the kids in the house.

Then she smiled. ''All right.''

He blew out his breath on a long sigh. ''Thanks. I appreciate this.''

Wanda led him to the door and opened the screen for him. ''You're welcome. And, in fact, I would be happy to provide baby-sitting services anytime.''

''Really?'' Deke said, grateful that this had been so easy, but not about to question his good luck. Accepting her silent invitation to leave, he took a step toward the door, but she caught his forearm and stopped him.

''As long as you don't hurt Laurel.''

The tone of her voice might have scared a lesser man. But because Deke was coming to understand that people from small towns took the business of caring for one another quite seriously and didn't cotton well to people they didn't trust, he looked her right in the eye.

''I have no intention of hurting Laurel.''

''See that you don't,'' Wanda said, then indicated with her chin that he should leave.

In the car Deke released a breath he didn't even know he was holding. He thought back to his experience on the golf course when he played golf with the ex-husband of a high-school girlfriend, and couldn't picture Wanda playing golf with Laurel's ex-husband. Actually he could picture Wanda playing golf with

Laurel's ex-husband if the man was in the market to be hit with a club.

Driving home, seeing children at play, women and men chatting over fences, and a park where everybody knew everybody else, he finally understood the big difference Laurel continually saw that he missed. Her life was intimate, personal. His was broad strokes, filled with semi-intimate relationships and things. Money, trips, vacations, homes, cars and trinkets. Hers was filled with people. Her children played with the children of the men she supervised. She went to church with her boss. At work there might be levels of command, but out of that factory everybody was equal. Their world was too small for anybody to get an attitude or to behave in a fashion considered dishonest. You couldn't have a secret. Everybody's laundry was exposed—literally—for everybody else to see.

If that wasn't intimacy, forced by close quarters and truth, but intimacy all the same, Deke didn't know what was.

He recognized he needed the intimacy and truth of her life, but he also knew she needed some of the "things" from his. She was a well-rounded, intelligent woman who would love the symphony, raise charity funds like a pro and bring life to his cool and aloof country club.

More convinced than ever that they weren't just made for each other, they were *good* for each other, Deke drove back to the plant just in time for the bell that signaled the end of the half-hour lunch period.

"Get your errands done?" Laurel asked as he stepped into the Shipping and Receiving cage.

"Actually I had only one errand."

She peered up at him. "That sounds mysterious."

Deke grinned. "It is, but right now we have bigger fish to fry. Do you think you can get two hours of overtime authorized for tonight so you can show me everything you discovered?"

"Sure," Laurel said. "No problem."

Danny Greene approached Laurel and handed her a clipboard, which took her attention, but Deke didn't care. Still pretending to be an executive trainee, he ambled back to his workstation. As far as everyone in this company was concerned, he had been gone for three weeks because of a family emergency. Now he was finishing up his stint in Shipping and Receiving, and on Monday he would move on to the Contracts Department. But if everything went right tonight, and Deke had no reason to believe it wouldn't, he would not only be returning to Pittsburgh Monday, but Laurel would be coming with him.

"What are you doing?" Laurel asked Deke when he bent down to help Sophie with her little pink bunny coat.

"I've arranged for the kids to have a baby-sitter tonight."

It not only confused her that he would arrange for a baby-sitter, it also puzzled her that he hadn't simply asked her mother to stay for the two hours they would be gone, instead of taking her home while Laurel was puttering in her bedroom.

"Why?"

Deke laughed. "Because we're about to leave, remember?"

"Yeah, remember?" Sophie asked comically, grinning as she held her bear over her head allowing Deke to zip her lightweight coat.

"Wanda said she would watch the kids," he added as he picked up Sophie. She immediately wrapped her arms around his neck, her bear thumping against his back as she did so.

"Oh, okay," Laurel said, grabbing her own spring jacket for later when she knew the temperature would fall. When Deke reached for Sophie's Barbie luggage, she asked, "Why are you taking that?"

"Wanda's keeping the kids for the night," Deke said just as Audra came barreling out of her bedroom.

"All set," Audra announced. "I have pj's, my schoolbooks and clothes for school tomorrow."

"Why?" Laurel asked, then trailed her gaze from Audra to Deke.

"Because the kids are staying overnight with Wanda."

"You already said that." Laurel crossed her arms. "What I want to know is why the kids are staying overnight with Wanda."

"Because we'll be getting home late."

"Not really. It's seven. If we work two hours, we'll be home by nine."

"How about this, then?" Deke said, shifting Sophie out of the way, then stretching to place a kiss on Laurel's lips. "I wanted a little time alone."

"Yeah, Mom," Audra said in exasperation as she rolled her eyes. "You two never have any time alone."

Caught between the shock of wondering just how much her little girl new about men and women and time alone, and the shock of realizing she would be spending the entire night alone—with Deke—Laurel didn't know which problem to address.

But it didn't matter. She didn't get the chance to address either. Deke carried Sophie to the door as he directed Audra out in front of them. Scrambling to catch up, Laurel marveled at how easily Deke had taken to behaving like the girls' father, and how wonderful it was to have someone organize things like getting everybody into the car, but even as she thought that, her heart began to flutter. Recognizing that he was a master organizer, she didn't have to think too hard or too long about what he had planned for them tonight. In a roundabout way, he had even given her a chance to consider it, get accustomed to it and be ready for it.

It.

The *big* it. He wanted to make love with her.

Her heart froze.

She couldn't.

She just couldn't. She wasn't ready.

If she had thought ahead to look for help or rescue from Wanda, Laurel would have been sadly disappointed, because Wanda appeared to be a coconspirator. Before Laurel really knew what was happening, the kids were happily ensconced in Wanda's home, playing with their cousins, and she and Deke were walking back to his rental car.

He opened the door for her. "Ready for this?"

Eyes wide, she stared at him. His blue eyes sparkled with warmth, even as the last rays of the sun found their way to his shiny black hair to make it even shinier. He was gorgeous. He was wonderful. She couldn't deny that she loved him. She couldn't deny that she wanted to touch him and taste him and be as close to him as she could be. But there was a part of her that knew that too many issues stood between them for a commitment, and making love was a commitment. Finally she said, "I don't know."

Deke laughed. "How can you not know? It's the whole reason I came back."

"It is?" She stared at him rather than climbing into the car. She couldn't believe she had become that important to him so quickly. That having sex with her was—

"Sure. Once you show me the path our suspected thieves took, I can get an audit team in here and get on with the rest of my life."

"Oh, yeah," Laurel said, then she did slide onto the car seat because she didn't want him to see her embarrassment or the confused expression on her face. She tried to think back to the conversations that led up to them being alone in this car, but everything was muddled. Positive she had imagined the sexual innuendoes, she relaxed on the seat as he drove to the plant. She used her key to get them in the back door, and then into the Shipping and Receiving cage.

Deke strode to the computer and turned it on, confirming for Laurel that he truly was concerned with getting the information he needed—which was the reason he'd come back. She almost groaned. Why was it she kept forgetting that he wasn't here exclusively for her, but to investigate a serious theft?

Relaxed because that solved one problem, Laurel tossed her purse, keys and coat onto her desk and crossed to him.

"Okay," he said, smiling up at her. "Show me how you got the information you got."

"You're going to have to go into 'utilities,'" she said and began directing him to see the information she had recovered while he was gone, including how she had tracked one specific purchase order. When she was done, she took him into Inventory and showed him that only the lesser amount of the order was accounted for in Inventory, in spite of the fact that the original green copy of the purchase order, which she had kept, showed a greater amount had been purchased.

"You're brilliant," Deke said, then pulled her into his arms and kissed her as if it was the most natural thing in the world to do.

In a way Laurel supposed it was. They were incredibly attracted to each other. Unfortunately the kiss took her back to her original fear that he planned to make love with her tonight. Even though the very thought sent a thrill through her, it also scared her silly. She really wasn't sure they were ready for this.

She pulled away slowly and reluctantly, but he caught her shoulders to keep her from leaving. "What else do I need to know?"

Because she was still focused on kissing and seduction, his question took her by surprise and made her wonder again if she hadn't misinterpreted things. She cleared her throat. "I ran out to get some milk one night—it was after ten—and saw Jim Franklin's car here. I also saw a light on in the plant. That probably makes him the biggest suspect because it proves he had an opportunity to take the things from Inventory."

"Very good," Deke said, then kissed her again. When he pulled her close, she melted into him. When he deepened the kiss, she let him. Playing a mating game with his tongue, she began to lose her sense of time and place, and indulge in the sheer pleasure of the moment.

"Anything else?" Deke asked against her mouth, and Laurel shivered.

Forcing herself to clear her head, she forgot to think it inappropriate that he would ask her work questions while raining kisses on her neck. "Not that I can re-member."

"Good," he said, then sighed with relief. "I won-dered how long it would take me to fog your brain enough that you would stop thinking."

"I can't stop thinking. In fact, neither one of us should stop thinking. This is a big step you're asking me to take."

She felt him smile against the sensitive skin of her neck. "How do you know what step I'm going to ask you to take?"

She pushed away and looked at him. "You're not trying to seduce me?"

"Not at all."

"Oh," she said, embarrassed again. She attempted to step away, but he hauled her back.

"I'm not trying. I intend to succeed."

Chapter Eleven

At that precise second, the night phone began to ring. Connected into the plant's paging system, the bell echoed hollowly through the entire factory.

"What the hell is that?" Deke asked, glancing around. "It sounds like a phone."

"It is a phone. It's coming through the paging system. Because people working overtime aren't always close enough to a telephone to hear it ring, this is the only way anyone can get in touch with them in case of an emergency."

The minute she said *emergency,* Laurel's mouth dropped open and her heart stopped. "Oh, God."

"Don't panic," Deke said, running to the extension hanging on the wall of the Inventory Department. Before he picked up the receiver, he said, "How do I answer it?"

"Star-six-seven," Laurel said, rushing to stand behind him.

"Hello."

"Hello, Deke?"

"Yeah, it's me, Wanda," he said.

"Is Laurel with you?" she asked quickly.

"Yeah, she's right here," he said.

Laurel grabbed the phone from Deke's hand. "Wanda, what's—"

"I'm sorry, Laurel," Wanda said, her voice shaking. "But Audra's had an accident." She paused and drew a long breath. "I think her ankle might be broken."

"Oh, no!" Laurel said. "Are you at the hospital?"

"We just got here."

"We're on our way."

"On our way where?" Deke asked as she hung up the phone.

"The hospital. Wanda thinks Audra broke her ankle."

Deke hustled her out of the Inventory Department. "Grab your coat and purse. I'll bring the car around."

It took them less than twenty minutes to get out of the plant and to the hospital. Because it was a slow night, Audra had already been x-rayed by the time they got there.

"Are you okay?" Laurel asked anxiously, stroking the silky hair on Audra's head.

"My foot hurts," Audra said sleepily, obviously having been given something for the pain.

"I'll bet it does," Deke said from the other side of the bed, looking every bit as concerned as Laurel. Audra turned her head and smiled at him.

Laurel stepped back. With the crisis past, and a moment to think, she remembered a few other things that needed handling. "Where's Sophie?" she asked Wanda, who was dabbing tears from her eyes.

"She's with your brother. All the other kids are

okay. Audra was trying to slide into 'home plate' in the rec room and ended up jamming her foot into the concrete-block wall, instead.''

"Don't be upset, Wanda," Laurel said soothingly. "I know accidents happen."

"Me, too," Wanda agreed with a shaky smile.

Laurel squeezed her arm in support. "You can go home if you want."

"I probably should. Sophie was really worried."

At the mention of her baby's name, Laurel glanced at Deke. "You know, it isn't a good idea for her to be away from home when she's upset."

Deke nodded. "You stay with Audra. I'll take Sophie home and assure her everything is fine."

"You don't mind?"

He smiled. "No, I don't mind, Laurel."

He made the statement kindly, but Laurel knew she had only gotten a temporary reprieve. Occupied with caring for Audra, she didn't think too much about the fact that Deke intended to make love with her. When the doctor arrived and announced that Audra had only sprained her ankle, Laurel breathed a sigh of relief. Not only could Audra go home, but also after a day of bed rest she could be back at school. Everything worked out the absolute best it could, until Laurel helped Audra hobble into the house on her crutches and Deke ran to the door to supervise.

Because it was after midnight, she had assumed he wouldn't wait up for them. But he had. She didn't know whether to be happy with his concern or afraid he had every intention of picking up where they left off when the phone call about Audra interrupted them.

"All right, Audra," he said, directing her to the sofa. "Just take it slowly and you'll be fine."

"Why don't we take her into her bedroom?"

"Good idea," Deke said, then he scooped the little girl off her feet.

She giggled sleepily. "I can walk."

"No, you can't," Deke said with a chuckle. "Just relax and enjoy the ride."

"Okay," she said, and snuggled against his chest.

Laurel's heart clutched. Her daughters had never had a father, and until this very second she hadn't realized how much they missed the little things. They had plenty of male influences in the form of teachers and coaches, and even Laurel's brother. But they had missed getting carried to bed, or sneaking around to buy gifts and plan surprises, or watching someone fix a faucet who actually knew how to use a wrench. Laurel had done all those things, some of them well, but in her heart she knew it wasn't the same as having a second parent. A parent with different skills and sensibilities who would deepen and broaden their experience and appreciation of life. Deke's skills and sensibilities were certainly different from hers and would certainly broaden their experience and appreciation of life, and for the first time Laurel considered, fleetingly considered, that maybe she was making a mistake by focusing on the bad parts of his life and ignoring the good. But in the end decided she was only kidding herself if she didn't recognize the bad far outweighed the good.

They tucked Audra into bed and she fell asleep almost immediately. Laurel tiptoed out of the bedroom with Deke at her heels.

"Did you get a prescription for something for pain?" Deke asked when they were in the kitchen.

She nodded. "I'll get it filled tomorrow."

"Okay," Deke said, then rubbed his hand across the back of his neck. "That's good."

Finally noticing his nervousness, Laurel asked, "What's wrong?"

Deke glanced around uneasily. "Can we sit in the living room for this?"

"It's that important?"

He nodded. "And I'm also that tired."

"Maybe we should wait until morning."

Solemn, serious, he caught her gaze. "We can't."

"Oh. Okay," Laurel said, then turned and walked into the living room, unnamed fear and apprehension stabbing at her. She sat on the sofa and he sat right beside her.

Without warning or preamble, he took her hand and said, "Tom Baxter will be here in the morning."

"Oh," Laurel said, then swallowed. In the excitement with Audra she had forgotten all about the plant and its troubles.

"After I got Sophie settled, I called him. I told him you had uncovered most of the problem while I was in Pittsburgh. I told him basically we were ready for the audit team to come in and find the specifics."

"Okay," Laurel said, so dumbfounded she couldn't think of anything else to say.

"He doesn't want to wait. He doesn't want to risk that somebody will catch on to who I am and what I could be doing and then cover his tracks. He wants to do this now." He paused, drew a long breath, then caught her gaze. "And he wants me to come home."

"I see," Laurel said, her heart stopping, her breath catching and everything in the universe coming to a crashing halt.

"I don't think you do," Deke said quietly, then

raised her hand to his lips. He kissed it softly, then said, "Roger is having bypass surgery in two weeks. That gives him and Tom time to get me up to speed on everything. It gives me time to get comfortable and allows Roger to go to his surgery feeling comfortable, too."

"It sounds like a win-win situation."

"In most ways it is."

Laurel couldn't help it, she was angry. On the road to furious. She had finally found a man who was perfect for her, a man who actually fit into her world, a man who adored her children and was adored by them, and fate was taking him away. "Why are you suddenly capable of taking over when two weeks ago you weren't?"

"Actually I have *you* to thank for that."

"Oh, don't thank me for that," Laurel said, then bounced from the sofa, yanking her hand out of his grasp.

Cautious, he leaned back and studied her. "I might have gotten the credit, but you were the one who found the problem with the inventory."

"So if I'm the one who found the problem, why are you the one who gets the credit?"

Deke chuckled. "Because I was smart enough to elicit your help. And I instilled enough loyalty in you that you investigated on your own while I was gone."

"It almost sounds like I should be the one going to corporate, then."

He shrugged. "Maybe you should." He paused, caught her gaze. "Except I'm the one destined to go."

His humility and sadness deflated her anger. "Yes, you are. I'm sorry."

"Hey, don't be sorry," he said, rising so he could

walk over to where she stood by the window. Gripping her shoulders, he turned her to face him. "I understand why you would be angry. It seems like we just really got to the place we both wanted to be and now I have to go."

She nodded. "That's part of it."

He held her gaze, staring at her intently, as if he could read her mind by looking into her eyes. "What's the other part?"

Smiling sadly, she said, "It doesn't matter."

"It does if it has anything to do with us being together forever."

Searching his bottomless blue eyes, she said, "I was hoping you could stay *here*. I was hoping I could convince you that you belonged here."

"Okay, let's run with that," Deke said. "Except we'll flip it around and have you and the girls come to Pittsburgh with me."

She stepped back as if he'd burned her. "Don't even joke about that."

"I'm not joking, Laurel. I want you and the girls to come with me. I need you."

As if to prove his point, he kissed her, but this kiss wasn't the soft emotional meeting of the mouths they had done before. This kiss was long and hard and hungry. With his lips and the hands that roved down her back, clutching her to him, he not only conveyed to her that he needed her, but that he was desperate to convince her.

Equally committed, she kissed him back, telling him that she needed him, too, telling him that she was as desperate as he was, begging him to stay.

But a kiss that started off as a communication of desperation blossomed into an expression of a different kind of need. Soon all the problems of their relationship disappeared, only to be replaced by a keen longing. She forgot that she didn't want him to leave. She forgot that he couldn't give up the destiny for which he had worked since childhood. She forgot that he couldn't stay. She only felt the need. Sharp. Real. Stronger than facts. More potent than tomorrow. This need tugged at her, pulled her away from sense and sanity and drugged her with desire.

It seemed to be the same for Deke. His normal reserve disappeared. He wasn't a clear-thinking future leader. He was only a man loving a woman. He was flesh and blood and heat and need. And for the moment he was hers.

"Stay with me," she whispered against his mouth.

"I can't," Deke answered, his voice raw with emotion.

His body shook, and Laurel suspected it was from his horrible conflict. He needed her. She needed him. But his family needed him. He needed to fulfill the destiny for which he had been raised. He was being pulled in at least four different directions, and the consequence was a bunching of his muscles and fire in his eyes. When he kissed her this time, it was with a hunger that defied description, and for a minute Laurel not only felt the swell of his destiny encompass her, she also believed she could make it in his world.

But memories of Sophie breaking the vase crashed in on her desire-induced dreams. She was bombarded by thoughts of Audra becoming withdrawn again as she had immediately after her father left. She knew her mother would be lonely without her. She would lose her job, her independence. Her children's lives would never be normal.

Shivering with need, aching with longing, she pushed away from Deke, pressing her lips together to keep from crying. "I can't live in your world. More important, my kids can't live in your world."

"They can adjust."

"I don't want them to 'adjust.' I don't want them to live in fear. I don't want their lives to be cold and closed."

As if absorbing that, Deke stood perfectly still. Laurel watched as he deliberately slowed his breathing. In his eyes, she saw him weigh his options and eventually withdraw.

"I see," he said.

She could hear the hurt in his voice, and though it mirrored her own feelings having him leave emotionless, strong in his own convictions, even angry with her was probably better for both of them. She took another pace back. "I don't *want* to live in your world," she said, emphasizing the word so there would be no misunderstanding.

"I got the picture the first time, Laurel," Deke said, then turned and strode out of the room.

Laurel collapsed onto the sofa and listened for the sound of his bedroom door closing. When she heard it, she bent her face to the tapestry accent pillow and let the tears fall.

Deke answered the front door when someone knocked at six-thirty later that morning. Then a man who looked like a retired drill sergeant with his yellow crewcut and broad shoulders entered the Hillman residence.

Deke immediately introduced him. "This is Tom

Baxter, Laurel," he said, pointing to the man in her doorway. "Tom, this is Laurel Hillman."

"It's a pleasure to meet you, after all these years, Laurel," he said, his eyes twinkling.

Laurel mustered a smile. After Audra's accident and then crying for another hour, Laurel knew she had only managed about two hours' sleep. She was tired and unhappy, and suddenly she didn't like this man who had been her "friend" for three years, because he was taking away the man she loved. Nonetheless, she politely said, "It's nice to meet you, too."

"I understand you won't be going to the plant with us today because of your daughter's accident," he added as Deke invited him to take a seat at the kitchen table.

"Yes," Laurel said. "Audra needs to stay in bed, so I thought I would take a day off myself."

"How did she hurt her foot?" Tom asked.

"Sliding into home plate," Deke answered before Laurel had the chance. "The kid loves softball so much that she convinced her cousins to play in the basement last night while their aunt Wanda was baby-sitting."

"How is that softball team, anyway?" Tom asked, the twinkle back in his eye.

"They're fine," Deke said, chuckling. "How about some coffee while we talk?"

"Coffee would be good. I've been driving for hours."

"Don't think I don't know that you paid off Artie Marshall so I could the coach team," Deke said, playing host by pouring the coffee himself.

Laurel took a seat at the table, too. Since Audra and Sophie weren't up, the kitchen was unusually quiet.

"I know you set it up so I would have something to do with my spare time."

"That," Tom agreed, taking the coffee Deke served him, "and the fact that your stepfather was looking for any way he could find to put you in a position of leadership."

Deke's eyes narrowed. "Are you telling me Roger thought my being in charge of twenty eight-year-old girls would help me manage Graham Industries?"

"Hey, leadership is leadership."

Deke chuckled. "I suppose."

"You did take that team to the finals in their division."

"Only because I persuaded Laurel's brother, Jeff, to fill in for me when Roger had his heart attack," Deke said with another chuckle.

"See, you convinced another person to help you. I rest my case for how your softball team proved your leadership. So, what do I need to know about the theft ring?" Tom asked, then looked at Laurel. "Laurel?"

Surprised that she would be called upon to explain, she nonetheless told the story of what she had found and how she had uncovered it. Deke began making toast.

"Do you want some eggs, Laurel?" he asked when she paused in her explanation.

"No, toast is enough," she said, then continued to tell Tom that she had seen Jim Franklin at the plant one night when she had run to the store for milk.

"Well," Tom said, obviously satisfied. "We'll leave the details and arrests to the experts. Everybody's computer is already being secured so no one can cover his tracks or erase data."

Laurel's eyes widened. "How is anybody going to get any work done?"

"No one is going to do anything today," Tom said with a light laugh. "The audit team is already at the plant. This is a theft investigation now, Laurel. We've called in law enforcement. Everybody will be questioned and the FBI will be drawing the conclusions from here on out."

"The FBI?" Laurel gasped.

"Let's not forget that people from Corporate can tap into your computer network using a modem. For all you know, somebody from Corporate headquarters, which is in Pennsylvania—another state, which makes this an FBI issue—could have done all this with an accomplice who merely removed stock as he or she was directed."

"Good Lord."

"It could be anything, Laurel," Deke said, placing her toast in front of her. "All we did was confirm the basics of what was being done."

"You mean all *Laurel* did was confirm the basics of what was being done."

Deke grinned. "Sorry."

"Don't be sorry," Tom said with a laugh, then rose. "Upper management always takes the credit for the work of people below them. It's part of our charm."

Deke laughed at Tom's statement, but Laurel noticed that Deke was dressed in a white shirt and tie with crisp navy-blue trousers, and he was reaching for a navy-blue suit coat. When he slid into it, he and Tom Baxter looked as if they were wearing an official uniform. She could imagine that when they walked into the plant to meet with the audit team and FBI, they would be a formidable sight. She'd bet her bottom dollar Loretta Evans would faint. Everybody in town was about to find out the real identity of the coach who had just about led this year's team to the playoffs. And some of them were going to be mighty embarrassed by it.

But she would also bet her bottom dollar Deke wasn't coming back. Filled with sadness, she stared down at her toast.

"Tom, could you give us a minute?" Deke asked.

Tom glanced from Deke to Laurel and then back again. "Sure. I'll wait in the car. Pleasure to meet you, Laurel," he said again, grabbing the doorknob.

Laurel smiled and nodded, then Tom left the kitchen, closing the door behind him with a soft click.

"Are you okay?"

"You shouldn't have made my toast in front of him," Laurel said, feigning a lightness she didn't feel. "He's going to think you're henpecked."

Deke shook his head. "Aside from having his support on the job, I really don't care what Tom thinks."

Laurel looked at him. "Well, I do. I'm not losing you to an empire that doesn't appreciate you."

"They appreciate me, Laurel. They'll treat me like I'm a god, because I hold everybody's future in my hands. You don't have to worry about me."

"And you don't have to worry about me."

"I know. I know you'll be fine," he said quietly, almost sadly.

She would have liked to tell him that though she could take care of herself, it didn't mean she wouldn't miss him. She would have liked to tell him that the ways she needed him had nothing to do with food and shelter, and everything to do with simple human want. She would have liked to tell him that *no one* would ever take his place, and that she would never love anyone the way she loved him.

But she couldn't. Not only would it make them both

hurt all the more, but also he had never said he loved her. In a sense, he hadn't even made the easy part of the commitment—by just saying the words. And if he couldn't do that, then he might not feel the same way about her that she felt about him.

"You don't have to lose me, you know."

She swallowed.

"You could come with me," he reminded her softly.

She shook her head. "We've been over that. I don't think so."

Suddenly, unexpectedly, he squeezed his eyes shut. "Why are you so stubborn? Why won't you even try?"

"I did try," she said, irritated that he couldn't see that. "It's not me that I worry about. It's my kids. Deke, just like you don't care what Tom thinks, I wouldn't care what your mother thought about me. I would work around it. But I do care what she thinks of my children. I do care that my kids would feel like less around her. I do care that they would grow up in that cold, sterile environment."

"Laurel, I grew up in that environment," Deke said, then combed his fingers through his hair. "Hell, I'll raise my own children in that house—" He stopped. His eyes narrowed and he stared at her knowingly.

Laurel swallowed.

When he spoke, it was with the disbelief of just having realized something that had been simmering just below the surface all along. "You don't want to come with me because you know that if you and I had a child, he would end up like me."

She winced. "Not exactly. The truth is, Deke, if you and I had a child, you and I wouldn't raise it. You and I and your mother and Roger and Tom Baxter and your maid and butler would raise that child. I couldn't handle that. Worse, I don't think a child should have to deal with that.''

"I see," he said coolly, stiffly, then reached for the briefcase he had stashed beside the kitchen door. "I guess that about sums it up, then.''

"I know that to you it all sounds selfish and stubborn, but if you would look at it from my angle—''

"Oh, please," Deke said, holding up his hand. "The bottom line, Laurel, is that our worlds are too different and our ideologies are too different. I happen to be proud of my family. I think they did a fine job raising me.''

With that he opened the kitchen door and strode out without saying goodbye.

Laurel swallowed hard. She didn't believe he liked his life. She didn't believe he liked the way he was raised. He was unhappy in that world but was forcing himself to conform because it was the "right" thing to do. He had never really had any choices, and the one choice he had—to change his life for her— he refused to take because he was trained to put his family first. Not a wife, not children, not even himself.

And *that* was the bottom line.

Laurel spent the day fussing and entertaining both girls, making a special supper and even playing cards with Judy. She kept herself occupied enough that she couldn't think about Deke, but when Audra and Sophie fell asleep, and Judy left, Laurel was all alone.

She didn't regret her decision. She had made it in the hope that Deke would see her point and change his mind. She had made it to save any children they might have from a fate like Deke's. She had made it for Audra and Sophie.

Realizing she would drive herself crazy going over

and over it, Laurel started up the stairs to clean Deke's room for her next guest. Not only was there no point in putting it off, but she wanted all reminders of him out of her life.

When she opened the door, she could smell him. The subtle scent of his cologne lingered in the air. His bed had been made. The dresser top was empty. Even the bathroom had been cleared of his toiletries. Still she could smell him.

Telling herself to ignore the sweet aroma of spice and musk and get moving so she could rid the house of painful reminders, Laurel cleaned the bathroom and dusted the furniture. She stripped the bed and vacuumed the floor. She left the windows open to clear out the scent.

When the room was completely clean, she felt she was in control again and happily made her way to the hall to retrieve the laundry basket holding the towels and sheets he had used. But when she lifted it and his smell drifted to her, she was flooded with the knowledge that he was gone. *Gone.* Probably forever. She would never see him again.

She fell to the top step of the hidden staircase, lifted the corner of his pillowcase and inhaled deeply. Even as his scent invaded her nostrils, memories of him, things they had done, how easily they had gotten to know each other, how easy it was to trust him, how well he kissed, how he made her feel—they all came rushing back. She saw every minute of their time together frame by frame. She saw the inevitability of their falling in love and the futility of ever hoping they could make it work.

Then she let herself cry.

Chapter Twelve

Deke walked into his new office and looked around. He was amazed that he was here, amazed that not only did he have the confidence to take over the corporation, but his family and staff believed in him, too, and amazed that everything he had "waited for" his entire life was suddenly his.

There had been no magic wand. Tom admitted they had taken advantage of Graham Metals' troubles to test him. But he had passed. Passed with flying colors. Not because he found the answer to the problem himself, but because he quickly figured out who to ask for help and wasn't afraid or ashamed to admit he needed help. In Tom's words, Laurel had solved the mystery, but Deke knew what to do with the information.

Thinking of Laurel, all the help she had given him, all the ordinary things she had taught him, all the feelings she had inspired in him, Deke felt the crush of pain around his heart, but he tried to ignore it. Laurel was right about not wanting to be here if she genuinely felt she didn't belong. He'd always known his was an unusual life. He had never considered it particularly difficult, though he had found it stifling. And Laurel wasn't making decisions for herself alone. She was also making decisions for her children. If she had only herself to take into account, he honestly believed she would have given his life a shot. More than that, she would have found a way to make his life better—in his heart he knew she would have made it exceedingly better. Since she couldn't, he didn't harbor any ill will toward her.

Unfortunately that didn't stop the hurt.

He sat at the desk, in the silent room paneled with dark wood and decorated in mostly browns and muted earth tones, and rubbed his hands down his face. Thick velour drapes kept out the sunlight. File folders littered the desk and the credenza behind it. His whole life stretched before him, bleak and dull. But he had expected that. He had never looked forward to that aspect of the job, but he had accepted it. What he hadn't expected, and what he couldn't find a way to gracefully accept, was that he now realized it would be empty and lonely.

He had seen how the other half lived, he'd come about as close to falling in love as a man could come without actually falling, and he had truly been himself for the first time in his life.

But he'd had to give it up.

Hearing her ringing phone, Laurel jammed her key into the kitchen-door lock and pushed her way inside. She assumed her mother had taken the girls out for a walk and dropped her bag of groceries on the table, then reached for the phone. "Hello?"

"Good afternoon," the pleasant female voice chirped. "Will you hold, please, for a call from Roger Smith?"

"Sure," Laurel said, shrugging out of her jacket. Because Roger's bypass surgery had been performed a few weeks ago, Laurel wasn't surprised that he could call her. What surprised her was that he had. Aside from the weekend she had spent at the Smith home, she hadn't said two words to the man.

"Hello, Laurel?"

"Hello, Mr. Smith."

"Now, I thought we agreed you would call me Roger."

Hearing the cheerful tone of his voice, Laurel let out a breath she hadn't even realized she was holding. Roger wasn't calling to tell her something had happened to Deke. The relief that flooded her nearly weakened her knees. But she pulled herself together quickly, because she knew there was a reason for this call, and it wouldn't do for anyone in Deke's family to realize how miserable she was.

"What can I do for you, Roger?"

"Well, for starters you could visit."

Laurel wrapped the phone cord around her finger. "I don't think that's a good idea."

"We'll put away all the priceless art," he coaxed.

"Yes, but will your cook serve something that my kids and I can pronounce?" Laurel countered, teasing him back and realizing the man wasn't so bad, after all.

"He will cook anything you want. Hamburgers, if you'd like."

"Let's not get carried away. Steak would be fine."

She expected Roger to laugh. Instead, he said, "Does this mean you'll come?"

Laurel took a minute to think about his request. She wasn't anywhere near to being over her broken heart or over the disappointment that the man who seemed perfect for her wasn't, but she was at least functioning like a normal human being again. She didn't cry herself to sleep anymore. She ate regularly. She no longer thought about taking up smoking.

There was no future for her and Deke, plain and simple. He couldn't change the course of his life. She couldn't survive in it the way it was. If she visited, all that would happen would be that she and Deke would be reminded of what they couldn't have, and the healing process would have to start all over again. In the end they would be more miserable than they already were.

"I can't."

She heard Roger's sigh. "Please?"

"Is something wrong with Deke?" Laurel asked carefully, fearful that that was, after all, the reason for Roger's call. But he was trying to get a sense of how she felt about Deke before he admitted it.

"No," Roger said quietly. "He's fine."

"Is he doing okay on the job?"

"He's doing very well."

"Especially for a baseball player, right?" Laurel asked, wincing at her boldness, but not quite able to stop herself.

"Let's just say we had our doubts."

"But you wanted him to be the one to run the company, anyway."

"It's a family-owned company, Laurel. All the stock is privately held. The truth is, if Deke had refused to run the corporation, the reins would have gone to his cousin.''

"Deke never told me that!" Laurel said with a gasp.

"That's because having Tony take over wasn't really an option to him.''

"Why not?''

"Our company prides itself on being an upstanding corporate citizen, and Tony's not as conscious of the necessity of obeying the rules as the rest of us.''

"Are you sure you guys aren't just being snobs?''

This time her audacity was rewarded with an appreciative chuckle. "No. Tony has had a drug problem. He's been married four times and he's already bankrupted three small businesses he started with money he got from the venture-capital arm of Graham Industries. We figure it would take him exactly six years to run the entire conglomerate into the ground.''

"Yikes.''

"Our sentiments exactly.''

"I guess I also see why Deke behaves so cautiously.''

"He's four years younger than Tony, and he basically knew that if we wanted it to happen, we could appoint Tony as the company leader. But he watched Tony blow his chance to take the reins not only because he was professionally incompetent, but also because of his personal behavior. Deke saw that he was the only person left to run the company when I retired, and he also saw that if he wanted to be the person to run Graham Industries, he couldn't be flippant about it.''

"And that's why he was so committed to being ready.''

"Yes.''

"I'll bet you hadn't wanted to retire for a few years," Laurel speculated, suddenly realizing what had happened. "But you unexpectedly got sick this spring and everything changed. You knew you couldn't wait for Deke to learn the ropes through trial and error in the off-season. You knew you had to bring him home because you knew you needed heart surgery."

"Yes," Roger quietly confirmed.

"So you brought him home and took advantage of our company's unbalanced audit to give him a trial by fire."

"Sort of, but—"

"But you had a heart attack before everything could fall into place."

"Yes, but—"

"You risked dying to make sure the corporation lived."

"Yes and no," Roger answered, sounding angry now. "Things aren't always black and white. I was playing the odds and I lost."

"Ever think it was the stress of your job that made you sick?"

At that, Roger laughed. "A few times. But, Laurel, Deke's a young man. I took over in my late forties. He's also a member of the family, not an outsider. He won't have to prove himself a hundred times a year."

"You already made him prove himself before you gave him the company reins."

"Only to make sure he was ready."

"And what about the rest of the family? Do they feel that way, too? Or will they be testing him every time he turns around? Will he have to follow their every instruction?"

"Deke can do anything he wants."

"You say that, but as far as I can see, he's stuck. Stuck making money for some guy named Tony to lose. Stuck making money for people who already live in the lap of luxury. Stuck baby-sitting the fortunes of a few aunts and uncles who could be—no, who should be helping him. Or else they should just butt out."

"I'm sure that's how it looks to you, but in an old distinguished family like the Grahams—"

Though she knew Roger couldn't see, Laurel shook her head as she interrupted him. "Don't give me that old distinguished family bull. I see it the way I see it because that's the way it is, Mr. Smith. Maybe this family has been doing things for so long that they don't even know how far off the mark they are. But it sounds to me like they are way, way off the mark. And it also sounds to me like they don't mind using one person until they wear him out—yourself included."

There was a silence, a long one. Finally Roger said, "I can't persuade you to visit, then?"

She shook her head again. "No. I'm sure of it now."

"Can I tell Deke I spoke with you?"

"You probably shouldn't," Laurel said, her blood beginning to boil. For a family that asked permission before they did everything and tiptoed around feelings with impeccable manners, they sure didn't mind using one of their own.

Deke walked into his stepfather's room and pasted a smile on his face.

"Ready for your walk?"

Roger harrumphed. "Do I have a choice?"

"Actually, no," Deke said with a chuckle. "But if you want, we don't have to talk business."

"Talking business is the only thing that makes

twenty minutes of walking in circles around the garden tolerable.''

"Fine by me," Deke said, then escorted Roger to the back door. Though they had been told Roger was recovering nicely and was required to get into a system of regular exercise, Deke couldn't help watching him closely, monitoring his every move.

"I'm not an invalid."

"I never said you were."

"You hover."

"I'm just watchful."

Roger harrumphed again, then began his slow but steady journey along the cobblestone walk that led to the garden. "Nice morning."

"Beautiful morning," Deke agreed.

"Bet you would like to be playing ball on a day like this."

The thought had crossed Deke's mind. "I don't have time."

"There's no law against taking an hour off every afternoon, or maybe taking an entire afternoon off once a week. In fact, it's good for you to take a break every once in a while. Maybe even a few days."

Deke peered at his stepfather skeptically. "I never saw you take a day off."

"I didn't have to. When I got the reins, I was already married to your mother. I had a nice life. Someone I loved to come home to. You need some time to find a wife. If you don't soon start going out with a woman or two, you'll never get married. Women are an important part of a man's life. A good woman isn't easy to find. You shouldn't lightly dismiss the ones you stumble onto."

"Mmm," Deke stopped the words that wanted to

tumble from his mouth and the thoughts that wanted to infiltrate his mind. He had found a woman and she didn't want his life. After a few weeks he didn't blame her.

"Aw, come on, Deke," Roger groaned. "Don't make this hard."

"I'm not making anything hard."

"Do you think your mother and I haven't noticed that you haven't said one word about Laurel since you got back? One day you're bringing her to the house, giving us the impression you're serious about her, then a few weeks later you don't even mention her name."

"Laurel and I are through."

Roger shook his head ruefully. "So I hear, though I don't understand why. She was perfect for you."

"I know that and you know that, but Mother didn't think so."

This time Roger out and out gaped at him. "Tell me you didn't dump her because of your mother."

"No, Laurel dumped me."

"Because of your mother?" Roger asked incredulously.

Deke shook his head. "Actually, she didn't like my life. She didn't want Sophie and Audra to be raised here, and she didn't want to raise any kids we might have here..."

Deke watched as Roger looked around at the perfectly manicured garden, the neat guest house, the green, green lawn that hadn't seen a weed in all the time either of them had lived here. Deke could almost see the wheels turning in Roger's head, as if he was trying to puzzle something out.

"I see."

Deke bobbed his head in acknowledgment. "Thanks."

"No, I mean, I'm really starting to understand things. This isn't an easy place for kids to live. But you could have gotten another house."

"Don't bait me, Roger. It was more than the house, and you know it. I'm the chairman of the board of a multibillion-dollar conglomerate. My days are packed with work. I don't have time left for a wife and kids."

"That's only true if you let it be true."

This time Deke gaped at Roger. "I saw how *you* worked!"

"Yes, but it was what I wanted. What I chose. I also didn't have kids. Mimi and I had you, but I could spend quality time with you at the office because you seemed to like to be there."

"I did," Deke conceded. "Sometimes I still do."

"So you really like the job and you really want to run the family company?"

"I guess."

"Don't guess, Deke," Roger said. "Be honest."

"Okay, I like the job. I like knowing that what I do matters. I like being a part of so much."

"So did I, but I also liked having a family, and you should have one, too," Roger said, then he paused. After a minute he said, "So aside from the fact that you work too much, what else was wrong between you and Laurel?"

"It was the whole package," Deke said, deciding to come clean. It felt good to get this off his chest. "The charity fund-raisers, our visibility in the community, no privacy for the kids, no normal life for the kids."

"You were fine in Maryland the whole time you worked there?" Roger asked seriously.

Deke nodded. "We were great."

Roger sighed. "Deke, I don't want to tell you what to do, but I will remind you that you run this whole shebang now. You can do whatever you want. You can hire more staff. You can promote Tom to vice president and hire an assistant for him. Underlings can take the biggest part of the workload. If you want, you can even live in Maryland."

"Oh, right! With the company headquarters in Pittsburgh, that's a little unrealistic."

"Don't be so hasty. I've been thinking about this," Roger said, then he grinned. "You're the only family member who can take over, right?"

Deke nodded.

"So, that puts you in the driver's seat."

"How so?"

"Who's going to fire you?" Roger asked, then he grinned again. "They can't. Deke, you can do anything you want as long as you keep the corporation solvent."

Deke frowned. "I would like nothing better than to promote Tom and give him half my workload, but there's no point if I don't have a life outside of work."

"You could have a life if you moved to Maryland."

"Like I said before, a four-hour commute to the corporate office in Pittsburgh every morning isn't very practical."

"So move it."

"Move it?" Deke asked incredulously.

Roger shrugged. "Sure. Build a building right by Graham Metals." He paused, glanced at Deke. "It's not like you don't have the money."

"No, it isn't," Deke agreed, suddenly seeing the merit in the idea. If he delegated half of his responsibilities to Tom, hired another assistant or two, he could have time for anything he wanted. If he moved the corporate office to Maryland, or even just his office, he could marry Laurel, he could be a dad to Sophie and Audra, and he could coach that softball team every year.

"You offer everybody who works at the corporate office an incentive package to move," Roger said, explaining some of the finer points of how to accomplish the deal to Deke. "Some will, some won't, but the company will survive. Corporations do it every day. And who is going to criticize? Aunt Bee? I don't think so. If she does, we'll threaten to put her son Tony in charge of the family's money and see how she reacts to that."

"But Pittsburgh is our home," Deke quietly reminded Roger.

"Pittsburgh is *my* home. Pittsburgh is your mother's home," Roger qualified. "It's our home because our friends and family are here. It sounds like your friends and family are in Maryland."

Deke licked his suddenly dry lips, seeing Roger's point but wondering if it would really be this easy. Power gave a man a load of responsibility, but it also had its privileges. He was the person who made the decisions. And he could choose to reevaluate any past decision and change it. He could, literally, do anything he wanted.

Roger stopped walking and took Deke's forearm to stop him, too. "Go. Go now while everything is in flux and everybody is expecting changes. Don't wait or you'll lose everything that matters to you."

It was in that second that Deke realized that though he wasn't necessarily going to uproot everybody from the corporate office, this wasn't something he could debate for a long time. He really could lose everything if he didn't make his choices quickly.

"Get your butt in your car and go to Maryland," Roger said, then turned toward the house again.

Tingling with the newness of the knowledge that he could make sweeping changes and really have a life, Deke felt an excitement he almost couldn't contain. The only thing that kept him from shouting for joy was his uncertainty about his ability to convince Laurel.

In fact, there was a part of him that was certain he wouldn't.

It was after lunch before Deke arrived in Maryland. When he did, he parked his car, strode to the door of the Shipping and Receiving bay and entered the building from the back without going through the usual protocols. He walked over to Laurel.

Apparently hearing a sound behind her, she turned, and when she did, she dropped the green purchase order she was holding.

"Hey," she said, sounding confused and surprised to see him.

"Hey," he said, slowly bridging the gap of the last few feet between them. "Audra in school?"

Laurel shook her head. "No, school's out for the summer."

"Is Judy watching the girls, then?"

Laurel nodded. "Yeah."

"Your house?"

"No. She likes to watch the kids at her house," Laurel reminded him, then she stepped back suspiciously. "Why?"

Suddenly Deke scooped her off her feet. "Because you're coming with me."

"Wait a minute. Put me down!"

"No."

He said it simply, decisively. And though Laurel didn't want to admit it, his taking charge thrilled her. Because she now understood why he was always so cautious, so careful, it meant a great deal that he would do something so silly.

Unfortunately this really didn't change things. "Wait!"

"No."

Realizing arguing was fruitless, she tried another tack. "Deke, this is ridiculous."

"No, it isn't. I'm going to marry you."

"You can't marry me! We've already been through this. We live in two different worlds."

"I'm moving into yours."

That stopped her. "Moving into mine? What about your family's company?"

"I'm moving it here," he announced casually, but he frowned. "Well, I'm not moving the entire company just my office and the administrative staff, so we can keep our town small…"

"You're moving your office?"

"Yes, and the top administrative staff."

"So you can marry me?"

He looked her right in the eye. "So I can marry you."

At first she was struck dumb, but realizing how serious he was, the facts came barreling at her. "Deke, we hardly know each other."

"We know enough. We know the important things."

"How can you say that?"

"I know I can't live without you."

As he said the last, he let her slide to the floor as if not wanting to take her against her will.

Staring up into his eyes, realizing she would lose him for the second time if she didn't do something, her sense of loss overwhelmed her again. The emptiness, the long lonely nights. "I can't live without you, either," she whispered.

He bumped his forehead against hers in relief. "Really?"

"Really."

"Good, because I was afraid this was going to have to get really ugly."

"How?" Laurel asked, then she laughed. "What were you going to do?"

"It wasn't what I was going to do. I was afraid you would argue with me."

"And you didn't want me to make a scene?"

"No, I didn't want to lose you." He paused, caught her gaze. "I love you, Laurel."

Laurel felt his words resonate through her. He loved her. He *loved* her. She knew their lives would never be normal, but knowing he loved her, actually hearing the words, changed everything.

"And you want to marry me?" she asked quietly, realizing suddenly that all her employees had stopped working and were watching.

He nodded. "I want to marry you. I'm going to hire an assistant for Tom, and Tom's going to take half my workload."

Something very much like joy began to bubble up inside her. "Really?"

"Yeah," he said, then grinned. "Hey, I'm the man now. The company will be run the way I want." He looked around. "You people get back to work."

At that Laurel laughed. "No one's ever done anything like this for me before."

"Maybe it's about time somebody did."

"I don't know what to say."

"Well, you could start by saying you love me," Deke said, exasperated. "I just decided to change about twelve family traditions for you. I'm going to move an entire segment of the company. I don't think a kiss would be out of line, either."

"You're right," she said, and propelled herself into his arms. She looked up into his handsome expectant face and said, "I love you. I adore you. I can't live without you."

"Thank God," he said, then kissed her, but as quickly as his mouth touched hers, he pulled back again. "By the way, who's been coaching the softball team?"

"Mr. Marshall. Why?"

"I want my team back."

"Artie was very happy with the five thousand dollars Tom gave him to sit out part of this season. I'm sure another five would get him on the bench again."

"Nah, I'll just make him assistant coach...or maybe I'll be assistant coach." He smiled. "I like that."

"Being assistant coach?" she asked dubiously.

"No. Being anything I want," he said, then kissed her soundly.

And Laurel knew her fate was sealed. From that kiss forward she was permanently attached to a man who wouldn't merely love her forever, he would also make her life rich with emotion and experience.

"What do you say we go for ice cream, then?" Laurel asked when Deke finally broke the kiss.

"Ice cream?"

"Yeah, we'll go get Sophie and Audra and take them to the windmill and see who's the first one to pop the question."

Deke's eyes narrowed in confusion, until he remembered that both of her daughters had predicted this marriage, then he laughed long and hard. He draped his arm across Laurel's shoulders and led her to the bay door. "My money's on Sophie."

Epilogue

"What's the matter with you, Ump? Are you blind?"

Laurel pulled on Mimi's hand and yanked her back to the bleachers. Dressed in red pedal pushers, a white tank top and white plastic sunglasses, Deke's mother didn't need to worry that anyone in Pittsburgh would recognize her.

"Really, Mimi, if you don't settle down, that umpire might kick you out of the stands."

"But the ball was over Audra's head," Mimi groused, fanning herself with a white linen handkerchief trimmed in delicate lace. "Surely he could see that. I saw it and I wear bifocals."

"Many umpires and referees should wear glasses, but they don't," Judy said, consoling Mimi with a pat to her forearm.

Audra took a good swing at the next pitch and almost sent the ball out of the park. Everybody in the stands rose to their feet, cheering. Mimi fanned herself harder as Audra rounded the bases to score the run and accepted congratulations from her teammates.

"How do you handle this?" she asked, giving Judy a suspicious look. "I know you're fifty times more protective than I am."

"I am," Judy said with a grin. "But I keep telling myself that Deke and Laurel's baby might be a boy," she said, pointing to Laurel's protruding stomach. "And if it is, he might play football, and if he does we'll need our strength for screaming at those games."

Mimi grinned unexpectedly. "Football? I'd never thought of that." She turned to Judy conspiratorially. "We'll tailgate."

"I can't drink," Judy said slowly, and Laurel held her breath.

For Laurel, it felt as if time stopped as Mimi quietly assessed Judy, then she said, "We'll bring ginger ale, then."

"That's the spirit," Judy said.

Laurel realized Deke's mother really had changed, just as Deke came running over to the stands to gloat about Audra's home run, but Laurel scrambled off the bench and caught him before he could reach the grandmothers.

"You've got to do something about these two."

Deke laughed. "I can't."

"You have to!"

"Laurel, you created this monster when you invited my mother to the first game last season."

"Yes, but I had no idea she would take to the game so, and then buy a summer house and be here for the entire season!"

Pressing his lips together to keep from laughing again, Deke shook his head. "I kind of like having them live here. Sometimes I even like having them at the games.''

"And I kind of like seeing this side of your mother," Laurel said, casting a wary glance at the stands where Mimi sat with Judy, no doubt plotting strategy. Beside them, Roger bounced Sophie on his lap and discussed the team with Tom Baxter, who hadn't missed a game since Deke officially became head coach. The fact that he sometimes brought a contract to be signed or letters to be reviewed in the seventh-inning stretch didn't seem out of place to the fans who treated the coach with a great deal of respect and even gave him privacy when he needed it.

Roger and Mimi had grandkids, Judy had found a new friend, the softball team never again had to worry about a coach, and Deke was happy.

But most of all, Laurel was happy. Really happy. Deep-down-inside-her-bones happy.

"You're right," she said, and smiled at her husband. "I like having them here, too."

* * * * *

Don't miss the reprisal of
Silhouette Romance's popular miniseries

**When
King Michael of
Edenbourg goes
missing,**

**his devoted
family and loyal
subjects make it
their mission to bring
him home safely!**

Their search begins March 2001 and continues through June 2001.

On sale March 2001: **THE EXPECTANT PRINCESS**
by bestselling author **Stella Bagwell** (SR #1504)

On sale April 2001: **THE BLACKSHEEP PRINCE'S BRIDE**
by rising star **Martha Shields** (SR #1510)

On sale May 2001: **CODE NAME: PRINCE**
by popular author **Valerie Parv** (SR #1516)

On sale June 2001: **AN OFFICER AND A PRINCESS**
by award-winning author **Carla Cassidy** (SR #1522)

Available at your favorite retail outlet.

Where love comes alive™

#1 *New York Times* bestselling author

NORA ROBERTS

brings you more of the loyal and loving,
tempestuous and tantalizing Stanislaski family.

Coming in February 2001

The Stanislaski Sisters

Natasha and Rachel

Though raised in the Old World traditions of their
family, fiery Natasha Stanislaski and cool, classy
Rachel Stanislaski are ready for a *new* world of love....

*And also available in February 2001 from
Silhouette Special Edition, the newest book in the
heartwarming Stanislaski saga*

CONSIDERING KATE

Natasha and Spencer Kimball's daughter Kate turns her
back on old dreams and returns to her hometown, where
she finds the *man* of her dreams.

Available at your favorite retail outlet.

Where love comes alive™

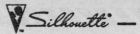

Silhouette ®

where love comes alive—online...

eHARLEQUIN.com

shop eHarlequin

- ♥ Find all the new Silhouette releases at everyday great discounts.
- ♥ Try before you buy! Read an excerpt from the latest Silhouette novels.
- ♥ Write an online review and share your thoughts with others.

reading room

- ♥ Read our Internet exclusive daily and weekly online serials, or vote in our interactive novel.
- ♥ Talk to other readers about your favorite novels in our Reading Groups.
- ♥ Take our Choose-a-Book quiz to find the series that matches you!

authors' alcove

- ♥ Find out interesting tidbits and details about your favorite authors' lives, interests and writing habits.
- ♥ Ever dreamed of being an author? Enter our Writing Round Robin. The Winning Chapter will be published online! Or review our writing guidelines for submitting your novel.

International Bestselling Author

DIANA PALMER

At eighteen, Amanda Carson left
west Texas, family scandal and a man
she was determined to forget. But the Whitehall
empire was vast, and when the powerful family wanted
something, they got it. Now they wanted Amanda—and her
advertising agency. Jace Whitehall, a man Amanda hated and
desired equally, was waiting to finish what began years ago.
Now they must confront searing truths about both their
families. And the very thing that drove Amanda from this
land might be the only thing able to keep her there.

THE
Cowboy
AND THE *Lady*

"Nobody tops Diana Palmer."
—Jayne Ann Krentz

Available February 2001 wherever paperbacks are sold!